Mrs. J. H. Riddell

The Race for Wealth

Vol. I

Mrs. J. H. Riddell

The Race for Wealth
Vol. I

ISBN/EAN: 9783337043483

Printed in Europe, USA, Canada, Australia, Japan

Cover: Foto ©Andreas Hilbeck / pixelio.de

More available books at **www.hansebooks.com**

THE

RACE FOR WEALTH.

A Novel.

BY

MRS. J. H. RIDDELL,

AUTHOR OF "GEORGE GEITH," "CITY AND SUBURB," "MAXWELL DREWITT,"
"TOO MUCH ALONE," "THE WORLD AND THE CHURCH," "PHEMIE KELLER,"
ETC.

IN THREE VOLUMES.

VOL. I.

LONDON:

TINSLEY BROTHERS, 18, CATHERINE ST., STRAND.

1866.

LONDON
BRADBURY, EVANS, AND CO., PRINTERS, WHITEFRIARS.

CONTENTS.

THE RACE FOR WEALTH.

CHAPTER I.

DUE EAST.

MANY years ago, in the dull cold light of a February afternoon, a stranger in London wended his way Due East through the city.

He was very young; he was very hopeful; he was very confident of himself; very sanguine as to his own future; he had entered the great Metropolis not an hour before, with the intention of conquering it, if such an expression be sufficiently intelligible; in the pages that are to come will be found the tale of his failures and his successes, of his faults and virtues, of his errors and repentance. Whatever of interest this book may contain will be centered in him and his; and for all these reasons it is fitting that the story which has still to be written should commence as he sets foot in London for the first time, and follow his steps till the chronicle is ended, and the volume closed.

It is a strange home which he is seeking; a singular locality in which he is about to pitch his tent — East, due East, in the Christian Babylon, in that great city whose inhabitants are as the sands of the sea-shore.

Will you trace his route on paper, most cour-teous reader? The way is not hard to find, even although your knowledge of London extend no further east than Gracechurch Street.

Perhaps, however, it is assuming too much to imagine that you can know anything of a street which is always full of vans and omnibuses; probably you have merely a vague recollection that the landmark I have chosen is somewhere in the city. Let me, therefore, refresh your memory as to its whereabouts.

From Charing Cross east you will find (if you consult a Directory map) a continuous line of streets running parallel with the river for a distance of a couple of miles or so; thus, commencing at the point above indicated, and marking out the way, child-fashion, with the tip of your finger, you have first the Strand; secondly, Fleet Street; thirdly, Ludgate Hill and Ludgate Street; then a sweep round St. Paul's; after that Cannon Street, the handsomest thoroughfare in London, though it *is* in the City; while, at the extreme end of Cannon Street, comes King William Street, which we cross at the statue, and which brings us at once into Gracechurch Street.

Were we to continue our route up it, we should, in due time, get into a truly delectable neighbourhood, bordered on the right by Spitalfields and Bethnal Green, and on the left by that strange land lying to the north of Barbican, and all round about Moor Lane, and Curtain Road. As it is, however, we turn our faces southward, and speak more fully of the territory in which we find ourselves.

Down there you perceive, slanting to the river, is Fish Street Hill, at the bottom of which runs

Lower Thames Street, a classic spot rendered sacred by Billingsgate, in which men knock up against the passers-by, with big baskets of fish and bigger boxes of oranges; where the air is literally foul with the smell of foreign fruits, for in Lower Thames Street oranges are more plentiful even than salt haddocks, and the side paths are lined with open shops, that seem overflowing into the dirty gutters, with nuts, and shaddocks, and lemons.

Yes, my dear madam, it is indeed from Thames Street, by Billingsgate, that many of the frutis you have at dessert, and the delicate lemons wherewith you season your puddings, are originally procured; it is from Thames Street that the cod-liver oil which the great Doctor Belgravia declares your consumptive daughter must either take or die, is to be had in its integrity; it is from Thames Street that the lemon and lime juice which you find so valuable in a sick room, make their way into genteel society; and it is from Thames Street that the bloaters the Londoners eat at breakfast, and the oysters they swallow for supper, and the salmon milor' has at a fabulous price per pound, and the turbot you order from your suburban fishmonger, are all had "first hand," as it is called.

Prawns, shrimps, soles, mackerel, salmon, trout, sturgeon, whelks, winkles, are all brought to Billingsgate—are all sold from Billingsgate—and scattered north, east, south, and west, on marble slabs, or costermongers' barrows, from whence they find their way to the dinner-table of his grace the duke, and to the four-o'clock tea of the housekeepers who live high up, next the sky, in city attics.

The piles of salt herrings and cart-loads of oranges, the great flabby cod-fish, and the equally sickly-looking "forbidden fruit," are enough to make one loathe the sight of food for a month—to say nothing of the dirty women and the drunken men, the elfish children and the shouting fishwives, the boys who will persecute one to buy flag baskets, and the respectable-looking old gentlemen who are racing to the railway station, carrying to-morrow's first course, in one of those identical baskets, home, the narrowness of the foot-paths, and the everlasting jamming-up of carts, and the swearing of the drivers, and the filth, and the misery, and the ecstasy of the street Arabs, and the pushing and elbowing required to force a passage through the impatient crowd !—verily, dear reader, this is a strange place in which we find ourselves—this Babel where the Easterns congregate together to cheat the Westerns if they can.

Leaving behind us Billingsgate, however, and proceeding eastward along Lower Thames Street, we get into a still worse atmosphere—into a locality redolent, not of oranges and haddocks, lemons and fresh soles, but of salt fish and rotten vegetables, and decomposing heads and tails.

Peep up that narrow street, or rather lane, for it is paved over the horseway, and opposite neighbours might shake hands from the top-story windows ; do not turn up it, for your nose' sake, but look up it, and try to imagine in what business the inhabitants can be engaged.

Through those basement windows whiffs of a terrible odour are wafted to the sense; glimpses are to be caught of baskets piled high, one upon another. You stand and look, and look again, and yet you are unable to tell me, as I am unable to tell you, what manner of men carry on business in this vile-smelling lane, with a sweet-sounding name—which swarms with children—where the gutters are full—where the air is foul—where fish warehouses abound—where the poor congregate together—where it almost seems as though human and animal life were striving together to produce a pestilence.

And yet the men and the women who have their homes here do not die quicker than their wealthier fellows; further, they love London, and would not go to live in the country at any price. They like to get among the green fields up about the New River and Hornsey Wood House on a fine Sunday in summer, or to go down the Thames as far as Woolwich or Graves-end, or to make their way down to the marshes beyond Plaistow when the proper season arrives;

but it would break their hearts to leave the city, for all that.

There are very strange anomalies to be met with in this region, and it may be that some of the *gamins* in Lower Thames Street love the smell of fish and sewage as you who live far away in the country love the perfume of the rose and the hawthorn. They may, when they grow to manhood's estate, have as tender memories awakened in their hearts by the odour of a stale mackerel or the sight of a mildewed orange, as are aroused in other breasts by the scent of the jessamine or the gift of a bunch of pale bluebells.

Spite of this possibility, however, it can scarcely be considered high treason to repeat the fact that the majority of the lanes, alleys, courts, and entries debouching into, and leading out of Lower Thames Street do stand grievously in need of a thorough purification.

I wonder if in this respect the East End be better or worse than in the days when all this neighbourhood was as genteel as lords, and ladies could make it, and whether the street lads now, are not in some matters better off than were the sons of earls and countesses then.

It is strange to think about nobility ever having lodged, clothed, and entertained itself down here; but nobility did hold great state east of the Monument once upon a time. It lived, it intrigued; it married in these old, old churches; the best in the land crowded the aisles of these now deserted buildings. Dukes and lords stood sponsors for the children of their friends and relations—kings and queens lived Due East in the Tower—plots were hatched in these dingy lanes—the oldest blood in England has dyed the ground in sight of the houses in Trinity Square. This is the part of London to which is attached the greatest historical interest, round which linger the memories of the most pathetic stories; youth, beauty, rank, valour, wit, royalty, treason, suffering, cruelty, romance,—all have the scene of their story here. The streets may be narrow, the air may be foul, the old buildings may be gone, the former inhabitants may be mouldering into dust, but what matters that? This is the stage where the actors played out their tragic or pathetic, or tyrannical, or loving parts; here the young gallants ruffled in their gay attire among the citizens—here the pageants swept by—here were priories—here lived the dignitaries of the Church—here the wealthy citizens had their fine houses—here kings pawned their jewels—here citizens insulted their kings. In the Tower, hard by, a Princess of Wales was kissed by the rabble; in the Tower Lord Lovat, the day but two before his execution, made that sharp answer to the Major of the Tower, who came to ask him how he did,—" Sir, I am doing very well, for I am fitting myself for a place where hardly any majors go, and very few lieutenant-generals." In the Tower were enacted such horrors as seem well-nigh incredible to modern ideas.

In these streets Elizabeth was exhorted by Noailles not to complain of the weight of the crown she was carrying for her sister. " Be patient," he said, " it will seem lighter when on your own head;" which no doubt she discovered five years later as she rode through London, receiving homage and congratulation while she passed along.

There is no part of London—none—so full of interest as this; and we may never forget that truth as we walk slowly over its stones, talking as we go.

Still slowly, over the stones likewise, Lawrence Barbour bends his steps Due East. He missed his way when he wandered so far south as Thames Street, but he asked the road to Limehouse from a porter, and is proceeding all right now.

He has not seen much of London yet; he entered it but an hour since, and walked straight down from the Great Eastern Railway Station,—or, as it was called in those days, the Eastern Counties,—to the street where we commence to follow him.

He has left Thames Street, and paced round the Lantern Church, and thence along Tower Street, and so on to Tower Hill. After pausing there to look at the Tower as it breaks upon him for the first time, he proceeds leisurely as ever across the square, and enters Ratcliffe Highway. It is not a nice route that he has chosen, not one a Londoner would select if he desired to give a stranger a favourable impression of the Metropolis, but Lawrence Barbour knows no better than to proceed straight through Shadwell to his destination. He is in no haste to reach that destination, which was the reason he elected to walk, instead of proceeding thither in a cab. The February wind is keen and cutting, the pavements are not over clean, the streets are not over dry, the evening is beginning to close, and the long night is drawing on the short winter day. The neighbourhood in which he soon finds himself is neither interesting, nor respectable, yet still he never quickens his steps, but, the first excitement of entering London over, walks on more slowly than ever, thinking of the great future that lies before him : of how fine a thing it is to be free at last to carve out his way in the world, at liberty to earn his own living,—to make his own fortune.

Hard and fierce had been the battle between the Barbour pride and the Barbour poverty, before he was suffered to try what he could do for the relief of the family necessities in business. The Barbours were great people, or, at least, they thought themselves so, and Mr. Barbour shed natural tears at the idea of one of his sons demeaning himself by entering trade.

When Lawrence first mooted the question, his father desired him never to mention such a project again; but, as the Barbour poverty became greater, Lawrence did recur to the matter, time after time, until at length he wrung a reluctant consent from the old "Squire," as he was styled, "to drag the Barbour crest into the mire of commerce,"—so Mr. Barbour put it.

"I should like better to drag the Barbour crest out of the mire of beggary," Lawrence answered stoutly, whereupon the old man declared, "That he was not a Barbour at all, that he was a Perkins, that he had cast back to the only low drop of blood which had ever entered into the veins of the Barbours since"——

"Since the first of our name trimmed the beard of William the Conqueror, I suppose," interrupted Lawrence; then noticing the angry flush that came into his father's cheeks, he went on,—

"What does our family do for us now? What is the use of blood without money? What is the good of birth unless a man have gold also? What is the use of being a gentleman if one cannot stoop without losing caste? I thought it was only parvenus who needed to be cautious about going on foot. Anyhow, I am certain of one thing, that no pride of birth will fill a man's stomach, and it is coming to want with us. I do not desire to run counter to your prejudices, but I will not stay here and starve."

"You are not asked to starve: your godfather wishes you to enter the Church."

"If I must be a beggar, I should certainly prefer not to be a clerical one," was the reply.

"And I have offered you time after time to write to my old friend Sir Charles Harrison, who would, I am sure, obtain a commission for you," went on Mr. Barbour.

"Could I live on an ensign's pay?" was the retort. "Could I live like a gentleman on an income no larger than a clerk's? Could I spend my life considering sixpences, and planning how best to keep out of debt? Look here, sir," and Lawrence laid his hand resolutely on the table; he did not strike it, because he was not at all of a vehement, impulsive nature, but he laid his hand down resolutely. "Look here, sir, I mean to leave home the day I am one-and-twenty. Shall I waste the year between this and that, or shall I go out and make money now? I will adopt either course you please; only tell me whether I am to stay or not, and let us argue no more about the matter."

Then the old man, looking away towards Mallingford End, towards the house, and the trees, and the lands, and the park that were his no longer, answered,—

"You shall choose your own future, Lawrence; you shall select your own road in life; and then whatever harm comes to you, will not be of my making; you may go into the Church, or the Army, or to London, or——"

Mr. Barbour's temper was getting the better of his parental feelings, so he prudently stopped short, and Lawrence replied,—

" I will go to London."

" Very well," said his father; " only, should you repent hereafter, do not blame me."

" I am willing to take my life on my own shoulders, and carry whatever burden I make for myself," was the reply. " Thank you, sir ; " and the young man's tone grew softer, and he put out his hand a little way, as if expecting his father to do likewise.

But Mr. Barbour answered,—

" There can be no unanimity of feeling between us in this matter. As you have decided to disgrace the family, be it so ; only you can scarcely expect me to shake hands, and wish you God speed on such an errand."

Before Lawrence started for London, however,

his father relented so far as to hope he would do well and keep well.

"And remember," were his last words, "while I live you can come home when you please. I will not shut the door on you, though you have disappointed me. Notwithstanding your low tastes, I have no reason to doubt your being my son." Having concluded which speech, Mr. Barbour turned back to the son who remained, while Lawrence walked out a prodigal into the world.

CHAPTER II.

Thus it came about that the young man entered London as described in the first sentence of this story, and walked Due East to the residence of the only relative he had in the whole of that great city, said relative chancing to be connected with him in manner, and fashion following:—

When the Barbours were really the Barbours of Mallingford End—wealthy county people with horses in their stables, rare exotics in their greenhouses, deer in their park, servants at their beck and call—Stafford Barbour, Lawrence's great-grandfather, married a Miss Perkins, daughter and heiress of Isaac Perkins, Drysalter, Crutched-friars, London.

The lady had plenty of money, which was in due time spent by her sons, Lawrence's grandfather being one of those who assisted in wasting the golden hoard.

All the gold Isaac Perkins had scraped together in the course of a long and industrious life took to itself wings and fled away, when the young Barbours came to lay hands upon it. Mrs. Stafford Barbour's fortune proved indeed a perfect curse to her descendants. On the strength of it they gambled, they betted, they trained horses that always lost, they purchased pictures—they married aristocratic paupers.

From the time Mr. Stafford Barbour brought home his bride, the race down hill began, and that race was only finished outside the gates of Mallingford End, when, ruined and soured, Augustus Barbour, esquire, widower, and the father of two sons, found himself with nothing intervening between his pride and the workhouse, save a modest homestead and a farm of some fifty acres, which having fortunately been settled on his late wife and her children, afforded a shelter, albeit an humble one, to the gentleman beggar in his extremity.

Had Mr. Barbour been a man possessed of one single strong quality excepting pride, he might still have done something with even the little territory which was left; as it was, however, he and his boys only lived, and but for the kindness of the rector and his curate, who, out of pure compassion, taught the lads gratuitously, Lawrence and his brother would have grown up totally uneducated.

All the day long, Mr. Barbour wandered round his land, or sat over the fire, reading books of heraldry, and those county histories which contained any mention of the former greatness of his family, and of the high people who had intermarried with the Barbours of Mallingford End. All the day the boys either studied or ran wild, whichever they pleased—Edmund Barbour generally inclining to the latter amusement, while Lawrence pored over his lessons, and thought and thought, till he was tired and weary, of the properties his ancestors had once owned, but which they now owned no more.

When the crisis of their affairs was publicly known there came a letter to Mr. Barbour from a very distant connection of the family—a certain Mr. Josiah Perkins—who, dating from Distaff Court, John Street, Limehouse, stated first the fact that he might be considered in the light of a relation, inasmuch as his father and Mr. Barbour had been third cousins; secondly, that having heard of the reverse of fortune experienced by Mr. Barbour, he thought it possible he might wish to put one of his sons to business; lastly, that if such should be the case, he, Josiah Perkins, could make room for a boy in his office, and would do his best to push him on in the world.

Mr. Josiah Perkins further proceeded to explain that he was a manufacturing chemist; that he lived on his own premises; that the boy could live with him on those premises.

Moreover—and Mr. Perkins evidently considered this the moral feather in his cap—his partner, Mr. Sondes, had a separate business altogether—to wit, a large sugar-refinery in Goodman's Fields.

It was a very straightforward epistle ; the letter evidently of an honest, well-meaning man, who knew nothing of the world—as Mr. Barbour understood the meaning of the phrase—who looked upon the "smash-up" at Mallingford End as he would have looked upon the bankruptcy of any very wealthy merchant, and who, having been all his life rather proud of the relationship existing between himself and the Barbours, felt that as a matter of gratitude for the satisfaction the connection had afforded him, he ought now to step forward and offer to do something for the family.

How this letter was received may easily be imagined. Mr. Barbour anathematised every Perkins who had ever existed since the beginning of time. He cursed his great-grandfather and his great-grandmother, and the drysalter and trade, and the city and Mr. Sondes, and Mr. Josiah Perkins, and all chemists and all sugar-refiners, and all presumptuous business black-guards who had the impudence to thrust their confounded shopkeeping under his very nose.

By dint of actual abuse he made the contents of the letter so public that Lawrence, whom he did not intend to see it, could have repeated the substance of the epistle off by heart.

Nay, he did more; he took upon himself to answer the proposal, which his father said he should treat with silent contempt, and at the age of sixteen entered into a clandestine correspondence with his relative, which never dropped, until four years afterwards the young man entered London, and wended his way due east to Distaff Court.

There was nothing romantic about Lawrence Barbour—nothing specially hard in the fact of his coming to London to seek his fortune. Money he had never owned; luxuries he had never known; good society he had never mixed in; and yet in so far as he had the prejudices of his class on many subjects, as he had not been born among business people, as he had not been trained to work, as he had never known what it was to call any man master, as he had not been brought up to labour, there was a something rather interesting in seeing how willingly he submitted to the curse of our race; how almost triumphantly he stepped forward and thrust his neck into the world's collar; how bravely he faced the fact that the choice he had made would harness him for life to the business car—would take him away from the hunters and the racers and the wild steeds of the desert, and turn him into a cart-horse, a drudge, a worker, till he had earned his rest, and was turned out, for the remainder of his days, into that green paddock, which is the *Ultima Thule* of so many merchants, and tradesmen.

It was growing dark when Lawrence Barbour found himself in High Street, Shadwell; but the gas-lights and the not over-reputable crowd that kept surging past amused his country eyes. There is a great charm in the gas-light; the London streets at night—that is, the streets where there are plenty of shops, which are full of the stir, and hum, and excitement of life—must always have a charm for a stranger. Take even the lowest neighbourhoods—take Whitechapel and Shoreditch, and the Hackney and Bethnal

Green Roads, St. John's Road Hoxton, John Street Clerkenwell, the Goswell Road, in fact any thoroughfare where the gas flames out from the butchers', and grocers', and drapers', and jewellers' shops—it would be impossible for a person new to London to pass through those streets without feeling both astonished and interested—astonished at the stream of human beings that flow ceaselessly along the pavements, interested by the light, and the bustle, and the life, and the unwonted aspect of the great city in which he finds himself. All at once it occurred to Lawrence that he might as well see how time was going; and accordingly he felt for his watch, but the watch was no longer in his possession. His chain dangled uselessly over his waistcoat; it had been cut, and the one solitary article of value the young man owned in the world was probably on its way to the nearest receiver's.

For a moment Lawrence stood still and looked back. He had some vague intention of retracing his steps—of tracking out the thief; but that instant, the vastness of London came home to his understanding ; the hopelessness of seeking for one man among millions of men was made plain to him, and at precisely the same minute there crossed his mind a doubt whether he should find the road to fortune so smooth a one as he had in his inexperience imagined it would prove.

He had come to London to conquer it, to make money out of its inhabitants, to earn a place for himself among the merchant princes of the Modern Babylon. He had walked along building castles and dreaming dreams, and, behold ! a hand had dexterously appropriated the one possession on which he prided himself, the one thing his mother had left him—a jewelled and most valuable watch.

Somehow he did not enjoy his walk so much after this little incident, and he enjoyed it all the less, perhaps, because he soon found himself in that end of the Commercial Road which is wide and dark and desolate by reason of its blocks of respectable houses that show few gas-lights, and all stand back disdainfully from the pavement. On till he came to Three-Colt Street, down which he turned ;—ten minutes more brought him to John Street, where an errand-boy obligingly informed him where Distaff Yard was situated.

"It's inside that there gateway," remarked the juvenile Londoner, "and if you ring at this here door somebody will come to you."

Having imparted which piece of intelligence the lad went off, swinging his basket, and whistling, "So you're going far away," which was at that time a popular melody, in the streets, as well as in the drawing-room.

Lawrence rang, and in a short time the door opened, and a man demanded his business.

"Is Mr. Perkins in ?" asked the descendant of all the Barbours ; whereupon the other answered that he believed he was, and that if he, Mr. Barbour, would sit down in the counting-house, Mr. Perkins should be informed he was "wanted."

As matters turned out, Mr. Perkins was in the counting-house, and there Lawrence found him seated on a high stool, engaged in looking over a file of accounts for some receipt or memorandum which he needed.

"What can I do for you, sir?" asked the chemist, pausing in his employment, and turning round to survey the new-comer, while he kept his fingers between the bills examined,—and the bills on the lower part of the file—a man of business in the minutest action of his life!

"I am Lawrence Barbour," was the reply.

"Bless my soul, you don't say so!"

Mr. Perkins doubled up one of the receipts to mark the page, so to speak, jumped off his stool, and shook his kinsman's hand till Lawrence's fingers ached again.

"Welcome to Limehouse!" and Mr. Perkins, still holding the youth's hand, stepped back a step or two, so as to get a better view of his face.

If the two had then spoken their thoughts, Mr. Perkins would have said,

"Well, I don't think much of the look of you;" and Lawrence would have echoed his words.

They were both disappointed. The chemist had expected to see a dashing young swell—a tall, handsome fellow—enter Distaff Yard; and when he turned round on his stool it no more entered into his mind that Lawrence Barbour was his expected cousin than that he was a prince of the blood.

He had rather boasted about this cousin to his business acquaintances. He had expected to find something above the common in a Barbour of Mallingford End, and now there stood before him a middle-sized young man, with lank black hair, with a pale face, with irregular features, with deep-set eyes, who talked with a slight country accent, and who had not the slightest pretension to being a fine gentleman.

Mr. Perkins did feel disappointed, but this disappointment made no difference in the heartiness of his welcome.

"I am right glad to see you," he said. "I hope you will make your fortune before you are as old as I am."

Lawrence, in his heart, hoped so, too; but he only thanked his cousin for his good wishes, and for his kindness in offering him a situation.

"Nonsense, lad," was the reply. "I mean to

have my value out of you yet. But now, come along, and let me introduce you to my wife and children;" and saying this, Mr. Perkins led the way out of his office and across the yard into the house, which was for a time to be Lawrence Barbour's home.

CHAPTER III.

TAKEN as a whole, Mr. Perkins' career had not been an astonishingly prosperous one. He had not done ill—but neither, on the other hand, had he done well.

Success is comparative, consequently men's views of it are different. Some are satisfied with a very small measure, others deem their object still unattained even when the bushel is full and running over.

Success to one is a living of five hundred a year, with a pretty church to preach in, pleasant society near at hand, no poor, and a good house; to another, it is a fair salary, a semi-detached villa, a strip of garden containing a piece of grass about the size of a table-cloth, a piano purchased by instalments, standing behind the door in the front parlour, a suite of walnut wood furniture covered with green rep, a dining-table, a set of spirit-decanters, and a cruet-frame, with various other articles too numerous to mention dispersed about the suburban mansion.

To a third, success is compassed when he has got his sons out in the world, and his daughters married or engaged. Up to that point there may have been a struggle, but for the future he sees his way plain, and binds the laurels of victory round his brow; while to a fourth nothing short of a title seems satisfactory, nothing under a patent of nobility worth striving for.

Success is what we make it for ourselves. The result of the social game, whether gain or loss, must depend, not on the opinions of others, but upon the magnitude of the stake that we have placed upon the board: and, therefore, when I say that Mr. Perkins' prosperity had been of the most moderate description, it must be borne in mind that I am gauging his condition by the ordinary conventional standard, rather than speaking of it as Mr. Perkins might often be heard speaking of it himself.

According to his own idea, he stood before the world a living example of the comfortable position any individual willing to work hard, may achieve without the assistance of a large money capital to start with. Lawrence Barbour's notion was, however, widely different to this. Mr. Perkins became in due time a living example to him of how long a man may walk through existence without making anything of his opportunities; and, allowing for the over-hopefulness of youth, for its impatience at delay, for its proneness to ignore the possibility either of failure or obstacle, Lawrence's view of the matter was sensible enough. There can be no doubt that, had not Mr. Perkins been so easily contented his success would have been greater; but then, he might not have felt so happy. So there are two sides to that question also.

He had worked hard—like a horse in a mill, he was wont to declare, when he talked about himself, a calamity of not unfrequent occurrence. He had not been extravagant, he had not been ostentatious, he had not squandered his earnings; and yet, supposing Josiah Perkins had died, his estate would not have yielded five thousand pounds net. Is this success? Mr. Perkins thought so, and was a very well-contented man; who never had any qualms of conscience as to the honesty of the trade in which he had embarked; who never, or at least rarely, regretted having left the more legitimate branches of his profession in order to engage in others which were, to use a mild term, questionable.

As the world goes, Josiah Perkins was a just and an honest man, and yet his trade was a lie, his business a delusion, every article he sent out of his yard a sham. Never a better fellow breathed than the manufacturing chemist; he stood by his friends, he loved his wife and children, he never forsook the people he employed when sickness or death entered their doors; but still, as I have said, his mode of earning money was not strictly legitimate, for Mr. Perkins was less a manufacturing chemist than a manufacturing grocer.

Had he not, however, been in the first instance a chemist, he could not as the years went by have turned grocer.

Science, experience, practical knowledge, all these were brought to bear—not on perfecting valuable discoveries, but on producing all sorts of rubbish. Nutmegs that had never seen a foreign shore; coffee-berries that had never grown on a tree; arrow-root extracted from potatoes; rhubarb useless as a medicine; pepper-corns made out of molasses and pea-flour; these were a few of the articles manufactured in Distaff Yard, and distributed thence throughout the length and breadth of England.

Doubtless there is no such thing as adulteration now; our tea is all from China; there is no starch in our ground rice; our raisins are not besmeared with molasses; our vinegar is free from all suspicion of pyroligneous acid; no trace of barytes can be detected in calomel; the bark of the alder-tree is never decocted into quinine;

glass flies are not sold for genuine cantharides; all the wine made in England is labelled "British," and would not dream of appearing at table in cut decanters, still less of being solemnly poured into coloured and frosted glasses by stately footmen;—everything men, and women eat and drink now, is, of course, pure, and there are no profits made illegitimately at this present time; but in the days when Mr. Perkins did business due east, matters were differently managed; some chemists did not profess to be particular, and their customers were less particular still.

If the grocers did well, the chemists did well too; if wages were good, and the poor flocked for little luxuries to the cheap shop in the main street—ay, and for that matter to the dear shops, too—Mr. Perkins' share of profits was satisfactory.

If, on the contrary, coffees, and spices, and farinaceous articles were not in demand, the half-year's balance in Distaff Yard was a thing to be wept over.

What would ye have, reader? The world is not all honest. There is knavery in the innocent country, as well as due east in London.

When in a facetious and confidential mood, Mr. Perkins was wont to declare, "There is roguery in all trades except ours;" and in the main, perhaps, Mr. Perkins was right. He was no more a rogue to the grocer than the thief is to the receiver. The latter knows the goods are stolen. The people who repaired for nutmegs made of bean-flour and grease, and coffee-berries made of bean-flour likewise, flavoured with coffee, knew precisely the nature of the articles they were buying. So far there was no deception, no roguery.

"I am as honest as any man in London," said the manufacturer. "I try to cheat nobody but the analytical chemists!" But then Mr. Perkins was continually trying to cheat those gentlemen; and it may safely be affirmed that he felt as proud of inventing any new process likely to delude them, as Watt did of his condensing steam-engine, or Arkwright of his spinning-jenny.

Into all these mysteries Lawrence Barbour was in due time to be initiated. As the years went by, he tried his hand at adulteration himself; but on that evening, when he walked from Mr. Perkins' office into Mr. Perkins' parlour, he had no more idea of the actual nature of the trade in which his relative was engaged, than you, reader, have of the best mode of extractig Prussian blue out of old boots and shoes.

By the light of the gas-lamp burning in the yard, he could see that he had travelled far to find a very humble home, in a very strange place; yet he was not daunted—he would not have turned back if he could.

He had chosen; and having chosen, Lawrence Barbour was not the person to let obstacles affright him, to permit small discomforts to influence his decision.

"My house is not quite so grand a one as Mallingford End," remarked Mr. Perkins, as he led the way towards his modest residence.

"It is a long time since we lived at Mallingford End," answered Lawrence, " and I did not expect to find a palace in Distaff Yard."

This reply, not being exactly the kind of observation Mr. Perkins expected, caused him to take rather a curious look back at his relative who followed him into the house, which was not much bigger than a good-sized packing-case.

"I hope, notwithstanding, you'll make yourself at home," said the chemist, hanging up his hat in the hall and motioning Lawrence to do the same; and as he spoke he threw open a door to the right of the passage, and introduced the new comer to his family.

Then for a moment Lawrence did receive a shock: such a small room, such a large family, such a paper, such furniture! He could scarcely help showing in his face some part of what was passing through his mind, and Mr. Perkins consequently volunteered the remark, that though the house wasn't a castle, still they were heartily glad to see him in it, and would do their best to make him comfortable.

"And when you've made your fortune and

have got Mallingford End back again, we will all go down and see you there, and talk about the night you first came to our little crib in Distaff Yard."

Lawrence Barbour laughed; the secret desire of his soul was to buy Mallingford End; but he was not going to proclaim that fact among these strange people.

"I have a notion," he answered, "that though the losing of Mallingford was an easy matter, it would prove a more difficult affair to get the property back again. At any rate, that is not one of the tasks I have set myself," and he shook hands with Mrs. Perkins, and, the civility seeming to be expected of him, kissed a variety of children who were seated round the table, each with a cup of weak tea beside it, and a wedge of thick bread-and-butter in its hand.

"Make yourself at home," Mr. Perkins repeated, and Lawrence accordingly essayed to perform this feat by "drawing up to the table," as Mrs. Perkins begged him to do, and accepting a cup of tea from her fair hands.

Let me try to sketch that interior as it appeared to the stranger's eyes.

A small room containing a large table, which left bare space for a dozen mahogany chairs, and a sofa covered with horse-hair; there was an old-fashioned grate piled high with blazing coals; there were two windows, draped with faded crimson curtains; there were Mr. Perkins in his office-coat, brown in parts with coffee, white in others with bean-flour, Mrs. Perkins, in a dark stuff dress, and five children, arrayed according to their age and sex in garments curiously fashioned, and evidently home-made—evidently, by reason of the bagginess of the nether habiliments of the little boys, and of the generally patchy appearance of the dresses of the girls. No one, looking even for the first time at the delft tea-service, at the children, and at Mrs. Perkins, could doubt the fact of the mistress of that household being a " capital manager," who had in a cheap sempstress, who affected char-woman, who washed at home, who liked grubbing in the kitchen, who locked up 'even the mustard-pot, and who, having a general idea that success or ruin hung on the saving or using of an extra pound of sugar a week, tried to do her duty, according to her light, faithfully.

While she was engaged in pouring out his tea, Lawrence employed himself in wondering where on earth Mr. Perkins had picked her up, and when he had exhausted his astonishment on that subject, he directed his attention to the eldest child, a girl of ten, who, seated opposite to him, was staring with all her might at the new arrival.

Miss Ada Perkins was one of those young ladies who would seem to be in great demand in creation, since nature turns them off by thou-sands; she was fair, she was fat, she had a broad face, a small *nez retroussé,*—not piquant in the least, but simply flat at the bridge and turned up towards the tip,—a large mouth, good teeth, light hair, in curls of course, with perfectly azure eyes, that possessed a power of opening wider than any eyes Lawrence thought he had ever seen before.

"Have you any more children?" asked the young man, thinking some observation on Mr. Perkins' small grapes would seem only polite under the circumstances.

"Do you not think there are enough?" demanded Mr. Perkins, who was seated afar off on the sofa, stirring his tea at arm's length from him; at which remark Mrs. Perkins laughed, and Miss Ada giggled.

"There would be quite enough for me," answered Lawrence; "but I did not know whether you——"

"Thank you," interrupted Mr. Perkins; "it is no such easy work to feed, clothe, and educate five children that I should desire any more."

"*You* do not know anything about such matters, Mr. Barbour," observed the lady; and once again Lawrence marvelled where his relative had picked her up, while Mr. Perkins answered for him—

"Time enough—he has his life all to come yet—and his fortune to make, and his wife to find."

Whereupon Lawrence mentally registered a vow that he would never find one like Mrs. Perkins.

At this juncture it suddenly occurred to the chemist to ask the young man whether he had dined, and upon Lawrence answering in the negative, Mr. Perkins became clamorous for cold meat.

"I'll get you a chop in a minute," said the mistress of the house—an offer which Lawrence won her eternal gratitude by declining.

"We have supper at nine," she went on; "but I am sure you must be hungry after your long journey. Let me get you a chop. Ada, run and tell Jane to——"

"Let me wait till supper, if you please, Mrs. Perkins," interposed Lawrence. "I would rather wait, indeed, if you allow me. I have been feeding on London to-day, I think," he went on; "at any rate, I know I have walked about till my appetite has gone," and forthwith he plunged into the conversational abyss, and told them how he had come on foot from the station, and asked about the places he had passed, and regretted the loss of his watch, which loss roused Mrs. Perkins' keenest sympathies.

"Was it gold?—dear, dear!—and oh, law! you don't say so—are you listening, Josiah? —enamelled and set with stones—I wonder you can talk quietly about it—it would have driven me mad to lose such a watch—look how the chain is cut," and Mrs. Perkins poised the chain Lawrence took out of his waistcoat pocket in her hand, guessing. at its weight and value. "Well, I never! it was a dear walk—what a pity you did not take a cab," and the chain was exhibited to the children, who, open-mouthed, contended for a sight of the gold, while Mr. Perkins, still seated on the sofa, looked at Lawrence, and tried to comprehend him.

There are such things as instinctive antipathies, and Mr. Perkins felt in his heart that he did not, as he mentally phrased it, " cotton " to the new arrival.

Why he did not care for the young man he

could not have told; but the antipathy was none the less strong because he was unable to trace its origin.

Mrs. Perkins, on the contrary, took a fancy to Lawrence, partly because he did not put the "house out" by taking that chop, partly because he had lost his watch, partly because he had had a watch to lose, and greatly because when she rose to leave the room he got up and opened the door for her to pass out.

"A most genteel, well-bred young man," she stated to Jane, in one of those moments of confidence that occur in the day of even managing mistresses, "and thoroughly at home already."

Which was true. Lawrence Barbour, seated on one side of the fireplace conversing with his relative, who now occupied a chair on the other, did feel thoroughly at home. Feeling at home is not always synonymous with feeling happy, so that is a part of the subject into which we need not enter at present. He talked, and Mr. Perkins talked, and the children disported themselves after a very quiet fashion (they were allowed to sit up for supper in honour of the stranger's arrival), and any person might have imagined that Lawrence had been an inmate of the house for the last dozen years.

Meanwhile, Mrs. Perkins was "on household cares intent" (when, indeed, was Mrs. Perkins not intent on such matters?), and the chemist had ample opportunity afforded him for studying his companion's character at his leisure.

"You are not in the least like the lad I expected to see," he said at last. "You are older, steadier, more manly, for your years, than I thought to find you. Do you resemble your father?" he asked, abruptly.

"No," answered Lawrence, who had a terrible knack of reading people's thoughts, and of replying to them, rather than to any form of spoken words. "The Barbours were all handsome. I am like my great-grandmother."

Upon receiving which piece of information Mr. Perkins broke out into a hearty fit of laughter.

"I suppose your father did not feel uneasy about sending you off to London by yourself," he remarked; "at any rate, if he did, he need not have done." And Mr. Perkins laughed again.

"Thank you for the compliment, if it be one," said Lawrence, gravely; and as the door opened he inwardly thanked heaven also, at the prospect of getting something substantial to eat, for he was famished.

"Long-wished-for come at last; isn't it, Mr. Barbour?" said Mrs. Perkins, pointing to a chair beside her, which Lawrence, nothing loth, took possession of. "Now I do hope you'll make yourself at home, and—oh, my goodness, Josiah! there is the bell, and it is Mr. Sondes, I'm positive. Now you'll see Mr. Perkins' partner," she added, in a confidential aside to Lawrence; and as she spoke, Mrs. Perkins drew up a little and settled herself in her chair, after the manner of a person who felt for the new comer no love, but much fear.

CHAPTER IV.

MR. PERKINS' PARTNER.

ALMOST before Mrs. Perkins had finished telling Ada to put down her shoulders, and Alfred to take his fingers out of his mouth, and Jessica to leave off rolling the tumblers "directly;" the door opened, and gave admittance to a tall man, who came in leading a little girl by the hand.

The assembled company Mr. Sondes honoured by a slight bow; Lawrence, being a stranger, he favoured with a surprised scrutiny. "That's the young man, is it?" he said, turning to Mr. Perkins; and receiving an answer in the affirmative, he told the new comer that he hoped he would like London and business; after which speech he sat down on the chair nearest the door, and began to talk to Mr. Perkins on the matter which had procured the pleasure of his company for Distaff Yard.

"Won't you have a bite of supper, Mr. Sondes?" nervously inquired the lady of the house—"a bit of mutton, or a mouthful of cheese, or——"

With a gesture almost of horror, the great man declined the proffered civility. "You know I never eat supper, ma'am," he said; "nor Olivine neither, thank you all the same." And the little girl, at the words, looked shyly towards Mrs. Perkins, and in a low, sweet, timid voice added, "No, thank you," but made no movement to come forward and shake hands, or be kissed, or anything. Silently she stood by Mr. Sondes' side, till Ada, equal to that or any occasion, slid off her chair, and going straight up to the little creature, began to embrace her.

That was a performance Lawrence Barbour never forgot: he laid down his knife and fork to contemplate it.

For her years, Ada Perkins had the thickest legs of any child with whom he had ever been thrown into contact; further, she had the clumsiest figure and the largest waist.

The fresh arrival, on the contrary, was slight and fragile, ·and when Ada put her fat red arms about her neck, and went through a ceremony of kissing and stroking the new child, who submitted herself to the infliction with the air of a martyr, Lawrence could have laughed aloud.

"Come with me, do," Ada whispered, trying to lead her victim off captive, and Mr. Sondes chancing to pause in a sentence at this crisis, heard the entreaty, and released Olivine's hand. "Come with me," repeated Miss Perkins, and she led the little girl up towards Lawrence, and saying, "Speak to him, Olivine, that's our cousin who has come to live with us," covered not merely Miss Sondes, but also Lawrence, with unspeakable confusion.

"She's such a dear, she's such a dear," and Ada executed a miniature war dance round her, and kissed Olivine again (who unceremoniously wiped the kiss away next minute), and put her arms round her neck, and looked uglier all the time than Lawrence had ever thought it was possible for a child to look.

"Will you shake hands with me?" he asked, and Olivine put out a little hand, and placed it shyly in his.

"How are the cats, Olivine?" inquired Mrs. Perkins, with an effort at seeming at ease, which signally failed.

"They are very well, thank you," and the child lifted a pair of lovely eyes—oh, lovely!—to her questioner's face.

"She has got two cats and a kitten," explained Ada, and Lawrence sincerely pitied Mr. Perkins for owning a daughter with such a face, and voice.

"And I have a dog, and a parrot, and four rabbits, and a pair of doves," added the child, taking courage, and addressing herself to Lawrence.

"And the doves say cock-aroo, cock-aroo, all the day long, and the parrot calls himself prutty Poll, prutty Poll, that way," mocked Miss Ada, opening her mouth wide, and settling her head down in her short neck, "and the rabbits go so" (making a feint of leaping), "and the dog comes down stairs bow-wow, wow-wow," proceeded the young lady.

"My dear." It was Mr. Perkins who spoke, and Mrs. Perkins immediately desired her daughter to hush, while Mr. Sondes rising suggested that he and his partner should repair to the office.

"We are only keeping Mrs. Perkins from her supper," he said, with what Mrs. Perkins called that spiteful sneer of his ; " and he knows," she added, after he and her husband had left the room, " as well Josiah never gets a comfortable meal in the day but this, as you do, I was going to say, only that you don't know it. But, however, he does know it, and two nights out of the three in he walks, and takes him away from his hot chop, or steak, or roast, as the case may be. I should like to give him a piece of my mind, I should," and Mrs. Perkins, who would sooner have marched off to Buckingham Palace, and given the Queen a piece of that undesirable commodity, proceeded to " cover down" her husband's supper in an access of virtuous indignation.

"Because he's the monied man he thinks we are all dirt," Mrs. Perkins was proceeding, when she caught Lawrence's glance, which fled swiftly from her to the little girl.

"Bless you, we never mind what we say before *her*," exclaimed Mrs. Perkins; "do we, Olivine?"

"No," answered the child, plaintively; but she raised her eyes to Lawrence's with a look which had she been older he would have translated into—

"I wish they did."

"You see, he never pumps and she never leaks," explained the lady, with elegant terseness; "that is one thing I will say for Mr. Sondes; if he is scornful he is not mean; he does not go behind your back asking questions and encouraging spies, though often as not I think he is so careless because he fancies we are not worth being curious about. Well, the Lord is the judge of us all, both great and small," finished Mrs. Perkins, a little irrelevantly, as it seemed to Lawrence, who was beginning to think that his relations made him feel very much at home indeed.

"Will you tell me your name?" he said,

turning to the child, who answered with that sweet gravity which seemed so charming—

"Olivine Sondes."

"Olivine—how singular, how pretty! It is almost as pretty as you are."

"Well, I'm sure; what would your uncle say to that if he was here!" exclaimed Mrs. Perkins, while Ada performed another *pas seul*, and laughed, and giggled till Lawrence could have choked her.

"I shall be the death of that brat, to a certainty," he thought to himself; but his further reflections were cut short by the entrance of Mr. Sondes, who, saying, "Now, Olivine—Good night, Mrs. Perkins," took the little girl into custody once again, and was departing without further leave-taking when, remembering Lawrence, he requested the young man to "step this way for a moment."

Greatly wondering, Lawrence walked into the hall, where, under the gas-light, Mr. Sondes surveyed him at his leisure.

He looked him all over, up and down, from his

head to his boots, and from his boots up to the hair of his head again.

Then—"You'll do," said Mr. Perkins' senior partner, the proprietor of many shares, of numerous houses, and of that sugar refinery in Goodman's Fields, already mentioned—"you'll do," and he held out two fingers, which civility Lawrence, as in duty bound, thankfully accepted.

"Let me see you at Stepney," proceeded the autocrat, and Lawrence bowed acquiescence.

To have heard Mr. Sondes' tone, any one might have supposed that Stepney was Carlton Terrace, and the senior partner a peer of the realm; indeed, in his ignorance of London, the new comer fancied Stepney must be some very fashionable locality, and Mr. Sondes a million-naire at the least.

"Don't forget, Perkins. I wish him to come over," the head of the firm repeated; and Mr. Perkins looked both surprised and nettled as he answered, "I will not forget; he shall go to you." Having received which assurance, Mr. Sondes departed, satisfied.

"That was more than he ever said to me," remarked Mr. Perkins, as he and Lawrence walked slowly back, after seeing Mr. Sondes safely out of Distaff Yard.

"Now I wonder—I really do"—and at this point the manufacturing chemist paused, having found at last a product which it puzzled him to analyse—"whatever he can want with you."

"It is natural that a master should wish to see his servant, is it not?" asked Lawrence; and this matter-of-fact solution of the enigma so astonished Mr. Perkins that he did not recover from his surprise during the whole of the evening.

"So, he's gone at last!" exclaimed Mrs. Perkins, when they re-entered the parlour. "Anybody, to see the airs he gives himself, would think we were all his slaves."

"This young man says Mr. Sondes is his master," observed the chemist, indicating Lawrence.

"And so he is, and so, for that matter, are you. I have come here to do what I am told, to learn what you can teach me. We may as well call things by their right names; and if I am not your servant, and if you and Mr. Sondes are not my masters, I do not understand English, that is all."

"There are not many Londoners who would care to speak such very plain English, then," answered Mr. Perkins; "and from all I have heard about the family, I certainly never expected to listen to it out of the mouth of one of the Barbours of Mallingford. You must be very different from the rest of your people, I take it."

"If more of my people had been like me, perhaps the Barbours might never have lost Mallingford," retorted Lawrence; on receiving which reply Mr. Perkins opined that some day he should understand his kinsman better, and his kinsman understand him.

"I want to do the best I can for you," he finished.

"And 1 will do the best I can for you," Lawrence answered, and involuntarily almost his heart went out towards this plain, business man, for whom he had already conceived a great respect and liking.

" Then don't let there be anything more about servant and master between you and me," said Mr. Perkins, grasping his kinsman's proffered hand. " We will work together if we can, and I'll teach you all I know; and I hope you will succeed no worse than I have done."

After the children were dispatched to their innocent slumbers—after even Miss Ada had (with much difficulty) been induced to relieve society of her presence—after the supper things had been removed by Jane—after Mrs. Perkins had retired for the night—the chemist and Lawrence sat talking together for hours, about Mallingford, about Distaff Yard, about London and business, and the money which can be made in business.

As a matter of course, Mr. Sondes' name would obtrude itself occasionally, and at last Lawrence asked some question about the senior partner, which led on to the further inquiry as to what sort of woman his wife was supposed to be.

"He never had a wife," answered Mr. Perkins; at which piece of intelligence his companion looked aghast and murmured—

"That little girl."

"Olivine. She's not his child at all; she is his niece; and a queer, old-fashioned little witch is that same Miss Olivine. They are both alone in the world, and they live alone together in a great house over at Stepney, where there is a staircase so wide you could drive a coach and four down it, and a hall so large you could turn the horses round. Ay, now, that is a singular establishment if you like; and there is a sad story hanging to it also. Mr. Sondes had a brother, a clergyman, and wherever they met her I don't know, but they both did meet Olivine's mother in some place, and both fell in love with her at the same time; but she fell in love with the parson. She had a fortune, and people said while she was fond of him he was fond of her money. Anyhow, they married, and a wretched life he led her, if all accounts be true. He drank, and he beat her; and though they had lots of children they all died when they were babies, all excepting this Olivine, who was born in the big house where she is now. I remember the night she came into the world better than I can remember last night. Mr. Sondes sent for me in a great hurry, and bade me bring one of those great west-end doctors back as fast as ever I could.

"'I don't care what the fee is,' he said, 'only, tell him the lady is dying.'

"'Lady,' I repeated, 'what lady?'

"'It's Olivine—it's my brother's wife—she was forced to leave him, he treated her so shamefully; and she has come to me; and the fool I have got in from the neighbourhood says she cannot get over it,'—and, if you believe me, he began sobbing like a girl.

"Well I went, and I brought back the great man; and before the next morning this child was born, but the mother was dead. I should not care to witness another scene like that," Mr. Perkins proceeded, after a pause.

"Had she been his own wife fifty times over he could not have gone on worse, and then all at once he settled down into the man you see him now. The child has never been away from him since her birth. He won't send her to school—he won't let her have any companions—he won't get her a governess—he teaches her everything himself, and takes her out with him wherever he can."

"But her father," suggested Lawrence.

"Oh! he died abroad; there is no one to meddle between Mr. Sondes and his niece now, and I confess I should like to see the person who would try to meddle," added Mr. Perkins. "It is a strange mystery to me," went on the chemist, "how it happens that so often men cannot marry the women they want, and women marry men who make them wretched,"—and he looked straight into the fire, which was now burning low in the grate as he spoke, while Lawrence fell to marvelling whether the office coat and the business manner of his companion covered any romance, whether Mrs. Perkins had been "first love," or love at all; whether—but here the chemist struck in—

"Some men when they cannot get what they want, take what they can get. Mr. Sondes has not done that, and I think it would be a wonderful woman who could induce him to marry now;" having finished which statement, Mr. Perkins rose, and, saying it was time they were thinking of getting to bed, led the way to a small room at the back of the house, where he once again expressed a hope that Lawrence would make himself at home. "I sent after your luggage, and there it is all right," he added, pointing to his kinsman's belongings; "if you want anything, don't be backward about asking for it, and sleep on in the morning till I give you a call. No need for you to turn out at six till you get used to the ways of the place." And Mr. Perkins departed; but he returned again in a minute, and, putting his head round the door, said, "By-the-by, does not Mr. Alwyn, of Alwyn and Allison, own Mallingford End now?"

"Yes," replied Lawrence, "and a confounded snob he is, too."

"He does business with Mr. Sondes."

"He may do business with Lucifer, if he likes, for all I care," retorted the young man, in a tone which told how much he did care about the matter.

"Ay, that shows what friends and capital joined can do for a man," said Mr. Perkins. "He is as rich as a Jew."

"And as insolent as a Christian," finished Lawrence. "Look here, Mr. Perkins," he went on, "I hate Mr. Alwyn, and I hate his daughter, and I hate every man, woman, and child I ever saw enter his gates; not," he added, "that I have spoken to the fellow twice in my life."

"That is a pity," answered the chemist, regarding the question from a purely commercial point of view, "for he could make a man of you."

"I hope to be one without his assistance," said Lawrence, shortly; and when Mr. Perkins left him, he sat down on his box, and looked over the prospects of his new life.

Many a time, subsequently, he recalled that first night in London, and the projects that then filled his brain. Many a time afterwards he could see a lad full of youth, and health, and hope, sketching out the story of his existence.

He had thrown off his coat and waistcoat, and in his shirt sleeves mentally fought the fight of years. He learned, he worked, he battled, he conquered, sitting there all alone in his little chamber! He recalled the events of the day— could it be only one day? He thought about his new home, and his new relations; about Distaff Yard, and Mr. Sondes; about his walk through London; about his father and brother; about Olivine, and Olivine's mother; about that large house in Stepney; and then he went to bed, and lay thinking through the darkness, till at length, thoroughly tired out, he fell fast asleep.

CHAPTER V.

ENLIGHTENED.

THERE is not much likeness between the words Stibenhede and Stepney, but there is less likeness between Stepney as it is and Stibensheath as it was.

Meagre enough are the materials out of which we have at the present day to draw our mental picture. Gone are the palaces, and the ancient mansions—gone the men and women, gone the green fields and the country, and the trees and the gardens; whilst concerning Stepney, history is more reticent than its wont, more provokingly suggestive, more irritatingly silent.

" Of great antiquity and of great importance ; " says an old chronicler. " Stepney was once," he proceeds, " the residence of kings, the seat of parliament, which was held there, and the place where the deans of St. Paul's had their country mansion, some faint remains of which are still to be seen."

These lines were traced in 1770. Even then the glories of Stepney would seem to have become a tradition, for the historian never tells us what kings lived there, when parliament sat, at what date Stepney was of importance;* even then the silence of the ages had settled down on the place, and though many wealthy and responsible citizens had seats in the village, towards which London was already creeping up, still an hundred years ago it was sinking in the social scale, sinking slowly and surely.

And now, Ichabod,—the glory has departed. There is no famous ground here—for we know not why or wherefore the place was ever famous; there are few good houses in the parish—alas! how small a parish it is now! Over the once pleasant fields the meanest and poorest

* Since writing the above, I find mention made of a parliament held at Stepney, by Edward I., in the year 1292.

streets conduct to more streets, poor and mean also.

The vaguest tradition—the most common·place reality! The few large dwellings that remain fail to carry us back to any time when either the great or noble lived and suffered. We connect no tragedy with the spot. Save that it is said Lady Rachel Russell retired here to indulge her grief, there is no pathetic interest, so far as we know, connected with the place.

Here, as elsewhere, tears have fallen,—hearts been broken, but man has kept no record of his fellow's grief; and for this reason man finds no interest in loitering here. He sees God's creatures struggling for bread, labouring in the sweat of their brows for money which is often·times sorely needed. He walks among the sternest realities of existence as he paces those narrow streets. The curse is made visible in a neighbourhood where vice, and poverty, and sickness, and sorrow jostle each other along the pavements. There is no best here now, unless, indeed, it be the shops filled with wonderful

finery and elaborate jewellery in the Commercial
Road. Where do these shops find customers?
Where?—Alas! this is an age in which if people
go hungry they must be clothed—in which——. I
must stop at this point and turn back to the
Stepney, Lawrence Barbour saw when he went
to visit Mr. Sondes on the day following that on
which we first made his acquaintance, walking
due east through London.

The part of the parish in which Mr. Sondes
lived a lonely and desolate life was not on
Stepney Green, or in Stepney Square, or Church
Row, or anywhere near the church, round which
there still lingers a certain though by no means
an exciting interest.

In a street ballad, which was within the last
few years popular in inverse proportion to its
merits, the author takes occasion to mention that
his heroine was not born in Westminster, but on
the other side of the water. I quote this statement in order to escape the charge of plagiarism
—for there is a certain similarity in the position.
Mr. Sondes' house was not on the north side of

the Commercial Road, but on the other. He did not reside anywhere near St. Dunstan's, but at the end of Stepney Causeway, close to the Blackwall Railway, and within a very trifling distance of Ratcliff Highway.

The house he lived in, stands six doors south of the railway, on the east side of the street, if my memory serves me correctly; and any reader who is curiously inclined and not particular can see the old residence, and get a bed in it at a moderate—too moderate charge; for the grand old mansion is now a common lodging-house, and up the staircases and along the passages tramp John, Tom, and Harry—free of the premises at so much a night.

Hamlet made some original observations on the uses to which the greatest among men may be turned. Who would not think of Hamlet in those old-world houses, from whence the glory has departed, and the former inhabitants also? What will your great country mansion be transformed into, twenty years hence, Sir John? Possibly, if it be good enough, into an asylum for idiots! Where youth and beauty, where rank and wealth have assembled, there will be long dining-tables surrounded by jabbering imbeciles. What would you? The world goes round, and the houses go with it.

They are here to day, tenanted by the great and noble, by the wealthy and decorous; and they turn up to-morrow, filled with the halt, the blind, the mad, the bad, the very sweepings of the streets.

Or else their place, like the place of their olden inhabitants, knows them no more; and this—like an ancient grave disturbed to make way for the remains of a new-comer—is, to my thinking, saddest of all.

In a book written not very long ago, I described a house with every room in which I was familiar—a house I loved; the house where Alan Ruthven lived and Hugh Elyot died. When those volumes were written, the old place was still standing, the old rooms were as large and bright and sunshiny as ever; the chestnuts budded in the spring, and stood stately with flower, and foliage over the water; from the upper windows a view was to be had across the marshes to Epping Forest. In all save its name, Marsh Hall, was a reality; and now— well, now there is a street through the mansion where those I knew so well lived and suffered; the gable end of Alan Ruthven's factory still remained a few weeks ago, but even that is now, no doubt, level with the ground; the chestnuts are cut down; the garden is covered with houses and bricks, rubbish and mortar; the pond is drained; the conservatory gone, and there is nothing — nothing left to indicate where the house stood, in which the men and the women whose story I told, lived out the most important years of their lives.

So the world turns round. How, before these pages are finished, will it be with another house, —with the old-fashioned mansion in which Olivine Sondes had spent all the years of her young existence?

The residence is in Stepney Causeway still; it is the same house; and contains precisely the same rooms as it did on the afternoon when Lawrence Barbour set out from Distaff Yard to find it.

"Keep straight along Narrow Street and over the bridges, and then ask," was Mr. Perkins's parting advice; which advice Lawrence following, he soon reached Stepney Causeway, which was a much more select neighbourhood in those days than it is at present.

Well-to-do people lived there then; men who have since prospered exceedingly were born in this street, which still, spite of time's changes, looks grimly respectable, with its solid houses, with its old-fashioned door-ways.

It was always dingy, however—always, I mean, within the memory of people living now. What it may have been at a remoter period we need scarcely pause to inquire. There was a park once, at the rear of the very house in which Mr. Sondes resided; fifty years ago the place was a suburb; it is now London. Caroline Street and Dorset Street have quite recently sprung up over the ground that was formerly paddock and garden. Over the grass-plat on which Mr.

Sondes' library windows looked out are built poor little brick tenements; there is no garden at this present time; only, alas! the place where a garden has been.

When Lawrence Barbour, however, having passed through that street where, on the south side, every second building is a tavern, with "fine view of the river," painted red upon blue, blue upon red, green upon black, had crossed the "bridges," and made his way from the side of the Regent's Canal Dock into the Commercial Road, and thence, after about a mile's more walking, found himself at length in Stepney Causeway,—there was an odour of aldermanic gentility still hanging about the place; it was quiet, but respectable; it was dull, but not vulgar. The feet that have since profanely trodden those staircases were then roaming in far other scenes. Have patience! we are standing, at last in spirit, with Lawrence Barbour on the door-step of that house which was once tenanted by Alderman Shakespeare. The door stands hospitably open at this present moment, but in the days I speak of things were differently managed, and after the young man had knocked, he was admitted into the house by an old woman, who ushered him into the back room on the ground floor, which was called by courtesy Mr. Sondes' study.

Nor, although " study " is a large word where-with to designate the sanctum of a business man, was the name altogether inappropriate ?

In that room Mr. Sondes both read hard and studied hard. The walls were lined with book-shelves up to the very ceiling, and the book-shelves were filled with the works of the best authors of former days.

For modern literature Mr. Sondes cared little. Like many men who have from any cause been thrown off the main lines of life to some of its tranquil sidings, he sought his friends in the past rather than in the present; in memory, and the writings of the immortal dead, rather than amongst living men and living thinkers. Except-ing books connected with the profession in which he was most interested, Mr. Sondes bought nothing new; but all the most expensive and most recent works on chemistry he purchased with avidity; purchased, and read, and mastered, and turned in due time to good purpose for his own benefit.

There were book-shelves in the deep recesses on both sides the old-fashioned fire-place; book-shelves covering the panelled wood-work dividing his study from the dining-room; book-shelves on the south wall behind the door, and book-shelves to right and left of the large window which looked out in those days on a pleasant garden well stocked with fruit-trees. Beyond the field was a small paddock, now covered by Dorset Street.

Drawn up to the window was a library-table, on which were piled books, pamphlets, manuscripts, and mechanical drawings; between the table and the fire was placed an easy, very easy chair, occupied by Mr. Sondes, who rose, however, when Lawrence entered, and greeted him with a cordiality that offered a striking contrast to his manner on the preceding evening.

Mr. Perkins had sent a letter over by Lawrence, and this letter Mr. Sondes proceeded to read, bidding his visitor find a seat for himself the while.

When Mr. Sondes had read every word of the epistle slowly over, he laid it down upon the table, and then began to interrogate Lawrence.

"How did he like London—did he mean to stick to business—to put his heart into it, in fact—did he want to make a fortune, or to grub on all his life—as—as—Mr. Perkins has done, in fact," finished Mr. Sondes,- staring at Lawrence all the time as a person might look through a window.

"I want to make my fortune," answered the youth; "a man can grub on anywhere, but it is not everywhere he can push his way in the world."

"And how do you mean to push your way in the world?" asked Mr. Sondes, which rather difficult question Lawrence replied to, by saying, "that he did not know—he had come to London to learn."

"And do you want to be taught—are you

wishful to receive instruction ? " demanded the other.

For a moment Lawrence hesitated ; he wanted to understand what Mr. Sondes was driving at before going too far in his replies, but after that moment's thought, he said earnestly :—

" Mr. Sondes, it was not to earn a mere living I resolved to come to London ; I could have got that as a curate—as an ensign—without, as my father puts it, losing caste. I may speak plainly to you, I hope, without giving offence," and Law-rence paused while Mr. Sondes, leaning back in his seat, with his legs stretched out to their full length, his elbows resting on the arms of his chair, and the tips of his fingers touching each other, nodded assent, and added, " Go on—say all you have to say—as though I had nothing to do with you—as though you were likely never to have anything to do with me."

" I cannot do that," answered Lawrence ; " it is precisely because you have to do with me and I with you that I venture to say what I certainly should not think of intruding upon any other person. I am going to work for you, and you wish to find out whether I am likely to work to any purpose."

"Put it that way, if you like," said Mr. Sondes; "say it will be for our mutual interest to understand each other perfectly, and go on. You could have been an ensign or a curate, and gained your living in either the church or the army, but you selected business because—I wait to hear the reasons for your preference."

"Because I saw that business gives, not merely a living, but wealth; and that wealth is power."

"Where did you see business give wealth, and wealth power?" inquired Mr. Sondes; and, simple though the question may sound, Lawrence found himself puzzled to answer it.

Like all young people, he had worked out a general theory from a particular case, and even while he felt perfectly satisfied of the truth and accuracy of his own conclusions, yet, sitting opposite to that cool, cold, clear-headed individual, he felt it difficult to give any reason which might seem sufficient to Mr. Sondes for the faith he held.

For the first time his answer drifted away from the question; for the first time he replied to one question with another.

"Does not England owe all her prosperity and greatness to commerce?" he asked; "and is not it an acknowledged fact that wealth is power?"

"Does not the honeycomb owe all it contains to the industry of that useful insect the bee, and is it not an acknowledged fact that honey is sweet?" retorted Mr. Sondes. "Let us go back to the point whence we started. We were talking about yourself, not about England; you said you had seen business give wealth, and wealth power, and I asked you where."

"Well, I saw it at Mallingford," answered Lawrence, desperately; "I saw a vulgar, illiterate snob buy the place where we had lived for centuries, and then I saw that snob sell Mallingford End to a worse snob; and I saw the whole county-side bow down and worship Mammon,

the rector's wife toadying to the first great
man's wife, and the curate bustling up to dinner
at Mr. Alwyn's, as though he were going to
heaven."

"I can quite believe it," said Mr. Sondes;
" but what then ? "

" Why then, Mr. Nott and Mr. Alwyn both
made their money in trade, and money enabled
them to buy Mallingford End."

" Well ? " persisted Mr. Sondes.

" Well," repeated Lawrence, a little nettled,
" does not that prove the truth of what I said ? "

" Not in the least," answered the other calmly ;
" you saw the men who had won great prizes in
the lottery of commerce ; the men who have
gained only blanks you have still to behold : as
well might you select a bishop or archbishop for
a type of ordinary church success, and say I will
enter the church because in it men are rich and
powerful."

" If success in the church were dependent
solely on merit, I should not perhaps be wrong
in doing as you suggest," answered Lawrence,

who, seeing the weak point in Mr. Sondes'
armour, was not slow in taking advantage of it.
"Business is the one occupation in which a man
may rise, no thanks to anybody but himself."

"Is it?" returned Mr. Sondes. "I am afraid,
if you exhaust the matter, you will find that even
in business kissing goes a good deal by favour.
You will see, if you look about you, that a millionaire is almost as rare as a bishop."

"But wherever one goes in England men are
to be met with who have made large fortunes in
trade."

"Yes," was the reply; "and every time you walk
through the London streets you will meet scores
of men who have failed to make fortunes in trade.
Take all the small houses even in a neighbourhood
like this. Take the miles of humble dwellings—
take the hundreds of thousands of men living in
those houses who are making off life hardly and
with anxious difficulty. If success were an easy
thing to compass, if wealth were a mere matter of
hard work and industry, all our business people
would be merchant princes."

" But many have not the money; and ——"

" And ' what one person has done another may do,' you were going to say," finished Mr. Sondes, as Lawrence stopped short. " True; but then the chances are ten thousand to one against that other. Probably there are few who have not started in life with precisely the same views and expectations as yourself. It is so easy to dream castles —it is so hard to build them.' People get so weary as the years go by, bringing nothing in their wake but failure or moderate success. So many qualities are necessary to ensure even comparative wealth—so many circumstances may arise to impede a man's course. He may have relations dependent on him—he may have a wife who drags him down—he may lose his health— he may have a swarm of sickly children—he may make enemies—he may have too many friends— he may find the business pace too fast for his powers, the race too long for his strength."

" Is there any use, then, in trying at all ? " asked Lawrence almost fiercely.

" Yes," was the answer. " There is use, at

any rate, in your trying, for you are young, well-bred, strong, determined, hopeful, unencumbered. If to these advantages you are willing to add knowledge, you may be hereafter a rich man, though I do not say so rich a man as Mr. Alwyn. He did not make his money over honestly, and I presume you have no ambition to become a respectable rogue. By-the-by," added Mr. Sondes, " you know of course the nature of the business in which we are engaged at Limehouse. Talking of honesty reminds me of our own trade there, which many people might not consider exactly the proper thing. We are adulterators: does that word shock you ? "

" I have not an idea what you mean by it," answered Lawrence.

" You have heard of food being adulterated. Well, we make the articles for adulteration to order: that is, suppose a grocer wants a lot of chicory, he comes to us, and we grind it for him ; or he requires a quantity of imitation pepper-corns to grind with the genuine article,—we supply him. Or, it may be, he prefers to sell

Bermuda arrowroot at considerably under cost price; in that case he has to apply to us for arrowroot made from potatoes. It is the rage for cheapness that induces a trade like ours: people would rather pay twopence for an inferior article than threepence for genuine goods. Quantity, not quality, is what they look for. The consequence of which is, that grocers must adulterate, and the grocers must be able to procure the wherewithal to adulterate from a firm like ours, where every ingredient used is perfectly pure of its sort, and harmless. We supply them precisely as the chicory importers supply us, each selling a genuine article of its kind. It is a snug trade, but at the same time some people might object to it; for which reason it is only fair you should know the nature of the business into which you are entering."

"But what has all that to do with chemistry?" asked Lawrence, whose face had clouded considerably while Mr. Sondes was speaking.

"Everything: it takes a first-rate chemist,

I can tell you, to be a good adulterator; and
Mr. Perkins is a first-rate chemist; so thorough
a one that I often think it is a pity he should
be wasting his talents in a little poking hole
like Distaff Yard. Had he married differently,
and that we had come across each other sooner,
I believe he might have made a fortune,—but
that woman! There is a saying amongst our
London poor 'that a man must ask his wife's
leave to get rich.' Remember the proverb, for
it is a true one. Don't go and marry a woman
who will keep you down in the mud all your
life. We dine at five. Olivine is somewhere
about the house; you might go and ask her to
show you her pets, whilst I finish my letters.
What I have said ought not to discourage you.
The world, full as it is, can always make room
for a pushing, energetic, ready man."

CHAPTER VI.

Mr. Sondes watched Lawrence out of the room with very much the same kind of expression as that a man might wear who looked after a horse he had some idea of buying. Then he drew up his chair to the table and commenced writing, while Lawrence proceeded to the next apartment, in which Mr. Sondes had said he should probably find Olivine.

She was not there, however; but the servant who had admitted him, and who was now engaged in laying the cloth for dinner, took him up-stairs, where, in the drawing-room, they discovered Olivine, nestled into the window-seat, looking out at Stepney Causeway.

"Your uncle promised that you would show

me your pets," said the young man, by way of introduction.

"Do you care about pets?" asked Miss Olivine, lifting her eyes to his, and reading him as children do.

"Yes, very much: I left a dog at home that I was as fond of as you are of your doves," he answered; but Olivine shook her head in dissent.

"I could not leave them behind me," she said; and of course that settled the matter.

"What was your dog's name?" Olivine asked, after a pause.

"Gelert. I called him after poor Gelert who was killed by his master. You remember that story, don't you?"

No; Olivine had never heard anything about Gelert, and instantly became clamorous for information.

"Tell me about him; please do—please— please!" and the little hands were clasped together, and the sweet face upturned to his with such an earnestness of entreaty that

Lawrence could not choose but stoop and kiss her.

"Show me your pets," he said, "and then I will tell you all about Gelert;" to which bargain Olivine agreed by taking his hand in hers, and conducting him into the withdrawing-room, so called, but which was really rather an ante-chamber, where, in an immense cage, Poll was engaged in the somewhat monotonous, but apparently congenial, occupation of swinging.

At sight of Lawrence the wretch paused in his amusement, and commenced shrieking out at the top of his hoarse voice—

"Who are you?—who are you?" and then he went off into a series of whispers and murmurs which Lawrence had no great difficulty in conjecturing to be curses.

The creature had been taught to swear in whispers, and although those whispers were almost inaudible, the effect was ludicrous beyond all expression.

"Poll, Poll—pretty, pretty Poll," cried out Olivine; whereupon Poll turned down one eye towards her, and, immediately becoming enthusiastic, screamed out, " Ol, Olly, Olivine," which last word seemed to Lawrence so perfect an imitation of Miss Ada Perkins that he began laughing.

This drew the parrot's attention back to him, and the bird thereupon grew furious. It flapped its wings, it flew up against the bars of its cage, it hopped from perch to perch, still shrieking out, " Who are you ? who are you ? who the ——" At which point it invariably became inaudible, greatly to the advantage of society in general and of his young mistress in particular.

" He is very funny, is not he ? " said Olivine ; " but I do not love him like the doves ; they are so soft, and so beautiful, and they laid an egg last summer."

This ornithological eccentricity seemed to have given Olivine such intense satisfaction, that Lawrence could only hope the performance might be repeated on some future occasion.

" It is getting too dark to see the rabbits," she went on. " You must come some morning, if you want to go out to them ; and now I have nothing more, only the cats, and I do not know where they are, except Flossy. Flossy has a green eye, and a blue one ; is not it odd ? "

She had the cat under her arm as she said this, and was ascending the stairs leading from the door opening into the garden to the hall.

With her disengaged hand, however, she suddenly arrested Lawrence's attention, and caused him to glance across the hall, in the very middle of which a tabby cat was standing on her hind legs, motionless."

" She does that fifty times a day," Olivine said. " Uncle does laugh so at her. I taught her to beg, and now whenever she meets me she goes up just as you see her. She would stand like that for ever so long, if I told her. Wouldn't you, oh ! you dear, dear old pussens "—and the child made a dive at the tabby, and securing her, carried both cats up to the drawing-room, where in the twilight she sat down on the floor at Lawrence's feet, and bade him tell her about Gelert.

In the dusk he told her that story; with the reflection from the street-lamps making strange lights on the walls, with the blaze from the fire illuminating the child's face, Lawrence repeated to her the legend of that faithful hound; but when he came to the end he wished he had not done so.

Down her cheeks came the tears pouring like hail; through her fingers he could see little pools of wet making their way; he could perceive how the slight frame was shaken with sobs—how fully the excitable child entered into the misery of the narrative and believed in it.

She forgot her cats, she forgot herself, she forgot Lawrence—forgot everything save " Poor Gelert, po-o-or—por-oor Gelert," as she tried to say.

Then he tried to comfort her. Did the memory of that scene never recur to him in the after days, I wonder? He raised her from the floor, and drew her to him, and kissed—he who had never owned a little sister—the bitter tears away.

"Olivine, my dear," he said; but the grief only grew more pathetic, and she buried her head in his breast, and cried there to her heart's content—cried till his shirt was limp with moisture—cried till she was tired, poor child, poor Olivine!

Then, half in jest, half in forgetfulness, Lawrence began singing to her—making believe he was hushing her to sleep—and in a moment the child was still.

Softly the song rose and fell—softly the young man hummed the old familiar air that had come to his memory. Scarcely articulating the words, he went through verse after verse, looking into the fire the while, and thinking of anything rather than of the child on his knee—of the place he was in. Softly, oh! softly the song rose and fell and then died away; and when it did so, Olivine dropped out of his arms, and, seizing his hands, kissed and fondled them in a sort of rapture.

"More, more," she said, "sing more;" and she sat at his feet, like one in a dream, while he ran through his little stock of songs to pleasure her.

Was it pleasure, though? was it pure pleasure for the little creature to sit with her lovely eyes filled full of tears, hanging on every note of the music as if it were her native tongue she heard spoken after years of silence?

This was what the lonely desolate life had done. This was what the system of education had effected. Under other auspices, influenced by other circumstances, the child might have been as thoughtless and as gay as children— thank God—usually are; but, as it chanced, the delicately attuned harp was strung up to its highest pitch, and Olivine could bear no excitement of any kind without the tears starting into her eyes, without her heart being torn and agitated.

For an organisation like this what was the future likely to hold in store for her? What? Ah! Lawrence Barbour coul.l not, even in fancy, picture the end to that story as he sat looking in the fire.

Before he had exhausted his string of ballads, Mr. Sondes came upon the pair. Perhaps music was not exactly an accomplishment for which he had given his new acquaintance credit; perhaps, the song awoke olden memories in his heart, for he stood in the doorway listening,—stood in the outer darkness, looking into the room where the firelight was flickering about the antique furniture and casting strange shadows across the portraits and pictures hanging upon the walls.

Never a human being had a softer, sweeter, more pathetic voice than Lawrence Barbour. People think a lovely voice goes invariably with a tender nature, and are surprised and incredulous when they hear of cold selfish men, and hard calculating women, being able to sing like the angels and archangels in heaven; but I hold, and have ever held, that the great gift of music has nothing to do with the heart, and that some of the most passionate and devoted beings who ever dwelt on earth have remained, so far as that power of expression goes, dumb, and passed into the next world mutely and in silence.

But, as I have just said, most people are of a different opinion, and Mr. Sondes, being of the majority, decided that Lawrence Barbour must be possessed of every Christian grace and cardinal virtue.

"It is very kind of you," he said at last, crossing the room and laying his hand on the young man's shoulder, "very kind indeed of you to amuse my little girl. I have often thought of having her taught music, but I doubt whether it would be good for her."

Lawrence did not answer. Standing up and looking at the firelight playing over the walls, he was thinking that, if Olivine had possessed any musical talent, her uncle could not have hindered her learning. For himself he could never remember the time when he had not sung. So soon as he could stand beside the piano, he had been wont to pick out airs for himself among the black and white keys; he had chanted forth all sorts of old melodies in the great rooms at Mallingford End; he had made the long corridors ring with the clear treble of his childish voice; he had gone about singing under the shadow of the oaks and the elms; and when he ceased to be a child his gift only changed in character, and settled down into the sweetest tenor conceivable.

To such an one the idea of "teaching" seemed absurd. If the child were to sing, she would sing; if she were not to sing, no art could make her other than a mere machine. She could appreciate music; she had given him proof of that; but appreciation is so far removed from talent, that as a rule talent cannot appreciate any talent but its own. Talent can criticise; it requires quite another kind of genius to appreciate.

Dimly Lawrence Barbour was groping after this truth as he stood leaning against the chimney-piece, looking at the old-fashioned cabinets, at the carved oaken chairs.

"I should like to learn, uncle;" it was Olivine who spoke, rubbing her head against Mr. Sondes' hand the while, after the fashion of a pet kitten.

"Then you shall, my darling." And straightway Olivine clapped her hands with delight, while Lawrence looked on wonderingly.

She was such a shy child, and yet so demonstrative—so quiet, and yet so enthusiastic—so patient, and yet so eager. Many a long year passed before he understood that phase of womankind, and when light dawned upon him it was too late. Yet, no ; for it is never too late on this side eternity to see truth.

Shortly afterwards dinner was announced. Olivine, young though she was, sat at table with them. An only child has many advantages, or many drawbacks, whichever way you please to take it ; and being constantly with grown-up people was one of those drawbacks to Olivine. Never a matron of fifty conducted herself with more solemn propriety than Olivine at table. The eternal fitness of things, more especially of the things on a dinner-table, seemed early to have taken hold of her young imagination, and to have invested her manners with a certain dignity wonderful to behold.

Mr. Sondes was a stickler for etiquette. Lawrence could perceive that fact at a glance.

Due East, and living all alone, he yet dined with as much ceremonial as any resident in Belgravia. When Mr. Barbour senior lost Mallingford, he lost his pride in externals also; and the meals at Clay Farm were oftentimes no better served than those in the most petty tradesman's house in Mallingford.

Like all those who feel that a fall in fortune has involved also a fall in station, Lawrence was keenly sensitive to matters of this kind, and the fact of everything in Mr. Sondes' establishment being done decently and in order increased his liking for that gentleman amazingly.

And this liking was reciprocal. The more Mr. Sondes saw of the youth the more his heart inclined towards him. A gentleman by birth, yet above the prejudices of his order; brought up in idleness, yet willing to put his shoulder to the wheel and work, as though it had been his portion all his life; independent, yet not impatient of advice; resolute, yet sensible enough to stand and hear what older people had to say; capable of forming and maintaining an opinion, yet thankful to hear the opinions of others; possessed of great talents, yet neither vain nor proud of them: surely these were just the qualities to attract the attention and arouse the interest of a man like Mr. Sondes, who had travelled almost the same path as Lawrence was now pursuing, with the same ardour, with the same hopes, years before; years and years before.

He said to himself, "Here is a lad, with about every element of success in him; a lad who, properly looked after, will become a great man some day;" and he conceived a liking for the youth straightway.

To a certain extent Mr. Sondes judged correctly; for Lawrence was pretty nearly certain to gain a prize in the business lottery, his new friend had spoken of.

And yet, with all this strength, there was much weakness. Amongst the seed-corn tares

were mingled; and unhappily it is never till
the grain springs that man can tell what the
field of any other man's life is going to bring
forth.

CHAPTER VII.

DAY succeeded to day, and Lawrence Barbour had been for two months domiciled in Distaff Yard.

The small sitting-room, the little bed-chamber, the mode of life, the very business itself, no longer seemed strange to him. It was the old existence, the idle hours, the lack of all occupation, the monotony of the weeks, the restlessness, the discontent which it now amazed him to look back upon.

How he had endured so long that state of mere vegetation, without hope, without excitement, without employment? was the question Lawrence continually kept asking himself; whilst every letter from his father contained the inquiry, "When are you coming home; are you not sickened of business vulgarity yet?"

"Those who look for nuggets," answered the youth on one occasion, "do not usually expect to find them lying about on the carpets of properly-ordered drawing-rooms, but are content to labour in the earth till they discover the precious metal."

"Those who labour in the earth," replied Mr. Barbour senior, "are usually unfitted to spend their money, when obtained, in drawing-rooms."

"So be it," returned Lawrence. "I will take my chance;" and he put his shoulder to the wheel in earnest, and worked as Mr. Perkins had never thought it possible a gentleman born could work.

He had taken his road in life on his own responsibility, and when a resolute man does this he feels that, let the way prove rough or smooth, he is bound, for his credit's sake, to make the best of it. Had his path led him over burning ploughshares, Lawrence would still have proceeded to his object. He was strong, physically, and perhaps that has more to do with resolute perseverance than most people are willing to admit.

He felt it no hardship to rise early and to labour late. None of the advantages of station had ever been his, except its leisure ; and leisure without money, society, or amusement, is apt to grow rather wearisome.

Looking back over the years, he could remember the few events that had ever broken the monotony of his existence.

Once he unearthed a badger, and spent a day compassing its capture ; another time he killed a snake, which he and his brother carried all through the woods of Lallard Park, and left at the head-keeper's lodge—a great snake, which stank abominably, and which, hung over the branch of a tree, kept writhing and twisting till sunset when the galvanic life left it, and all was quiet.

Lord Lallard came riding up to the Clay Farm two days afterwards, to ask Lawrence where he found the reptile, and how he killed it ; and on the strength of this visit Mr. Barbour bemoaned himself for weeks, and lamented exceedingly when he enlarged on how intimate his father and the late Lord Lallard had been.

"Like brothers," finished Mr. Barbour, "like brothers; and his son would not have called here now, only to inquire about the snake."

Then he broke out and told Lawrence he would not have him trespassing on other people's domains.

"I was strict enough myself once," whined the gentleman-pauper, "and I won't have my boys behaving themselves like common vagrants."

Whereupon Lawrence thought it was quite as well his father did not know he had in former days been in the habit of going poaching on Lord Lallard's property. The Barbours had not fallen from their high estate with a mighty crash. They had not gone out like rockets—after blaze and brilliance subsiding into sudden darkness. They had not given up Mallingford without a struggle, and that very struggle had done more to lower them socially than their poverty. The land was let off, the covers were rented out to strangers, there were many shifts resorted to, many expedients adopted, before Mr. Barbour allowed the property to pass away from him and his irrevocably. He saved as carefully as he had once spent liberally, and the consequence was, that even before he and his boys sought shelter in the Clay Farm, they were looked upon by the county as Barbours of Mallingford no longer.

Lawrence himself could not recollect the time when he had ever received much respect from any one, or reflected upon the state in which it had pleased God to place him, with either pride or satisfaction; while as he grew up, seeing how much the world is influenced by appearances, he felt angry with himself for having done many things which were by no means orthodox and proper, and vexed at his father for having let him, and his brother run wild like young colts about the country.

All his pleasures had been stolen, and that

made them seem none the sweeter when he came
to look back upon them in after-life.

Was there any happiness now in thinking of
the game he had snared in Lord Lallard's woods,
of the surreptitious fires he and his brother had
kindled with stolen sticks on common ground, in
bye lanes and roads that were little traversed ?

They had never managed to hit the happy
medium in their cookery; the birds were either
burnt to cinders, or came out of their clay moulds
almost raw; yet there had been a keen enjoy-
ment felt in tearing them limb from limb, and
eating them all in a panic which Lawrence, in
his maturer years, was perfectly unable to comprehend.

Only he knew that whenever he heard in church
about the Israelites, he always thought of that
food which he had been wont to swallow in such
anxious haste, and he remembered likewise a
terrible hour which came to him when he was,
at thirteen years of age, prowling about Lord
Lallard's grounds, seeking what he could destroy.

The old lord was lying dead up at the house,

and Lawrence, who never poached on the Mallingford property, considered that, an especially
suitable and safe time for attacking the enemy's
outposts with an old gun, a canister full of shot,
and a powder-flask. He knew the gamekeepers
would be off duty, and so he went boldly and
popped at a pheasant.

The pheasant escaped, but not so Lawrence;
who was about to load again, when the new lord
laid his hand on his shoulder, and asked him
who he was, and what he did there.

"I am a son of Mr. Barbour, of Mallingford
End," answered the boy boldly, though he was
quaking with fear all the time.

"Well, then, come back with me to your
father, and we will hear what he has got to say
to all this," said my lord; whereupon Lawrence
besought his lordship to let him off. He offered
him his gun, his canister, and his powder-flask.
He turned out his pockets, and tried to bribe
Lord Lallard with the contents. Crying bitterly,
he held out to him in succession a knife with a
broken blade, a bit of slate pencil, three half-

pennies, one of them bad, a bullet, a piece of twine, a handkerchief, the thong of a whip, an old dog-collar, a battered tooth-pick, an apple with a piece bitten out of it, an old clasp purse containing some foreign coins and a shilling, some crumbs of biscuit, a song-book, dog-eared and dirty, a few marbles, a lump of cobbler's wax, a morsel of putty, a gimlet without a point, and a rusty screw.

"I have nothing else I can give you," sobbed out Lawrence, "except my watch, and I cannot give you that because it was my mother's, and my father keeps it locked up; but when I am a man I will pay you all I owe you, if you will only let me go now."

But my lord stood gravely holding the treasures the boy had forced upon him in one hand, while he still with the other retained his hold of Lawrence's jacket.

"You may keep them all," pleaded the lad, eyeing wistfully the while his gimlet and the dog-collar.

Then Lord Lallard, looking down at the

curiosities, burst out laughing, and laughed till the woods rang again.

"I tell you what it is, Master Lawrence Bar- bour," he said at last, "you will come to the gallows if you don't take care ; poachers are thieves, and thieves often grow into murderers ; do you understand, sir, are you attending to me ? "

"Ye—e—s," answered Lawrence, and then he began laughing too, for he saw his lordship was going to let him off, and he was vowing to him- self that he never would set foot in Lallard Woods again.

"You will get yourself into trouble," went on the great man. "You may be shot, or you may shoot somebody—likely to do one as the other with that old blunderbuss you have in your hand. If you get leave from your father, come to my head-keeper and ask him to take you out; I'll tell him to have a care of you—but, bless my soul, haven't you game enough of your own at Mallingford without poaching on my manors ? " he added, with a sudden recollection of the woods surrounding Mallingford End.

Then Lawrence told him—how the game was not theirs; how the land was let off; how he and his brother were not sent to school. In the fullness of his gratitude he made ample confession as to the snipes and woodcocks and pheasants he and his brother had captured and eaten; which revelation did not tend to raise the character of his keepers for vigilance in Lord Lallard's eyes.

"But I will never snare another," finished Lawrence, looking back sorrowfully towards the woods wherein he had spent so many happy days. "I never will, indeed; nor shoot one either."

"Come and ask leave of me or my keepers, and you may shoot as many as you like," answered his lordship; but Lawrence shook his head.

"My father would not let me," he said; and he went on very mournfully to the great avenue, where Lord Lallard bade him good-bye, and saying, "Be an honest, straightforward lad," tipped him a sovereign.

Which Lawrence, with his cheeks on fire, and his heart thumping against his ribs, put back into my lord's hand, thanking him for it, but he had rather not—he had rather not, indeed.

"Do you care for sovereigns so little?" asked the other, thinking of the foreign coins, and the halfpennies, and the marbles.

"I should care for them if I had them of my own," was the reply; "but I do not like to have money given to me, thank you, sir," added the boy, deprecatingly, for he felt in his heart he was seeming ungrateful and ungracious, and he had not heart enough to put any polish on his words.

"You are right, my lad," said Lord Lallard, "and I was wrong;" and with a friendly nod he turned away, never to meet Lawrence again till the latter, five years afterwards, roaming with his brother through Lallard Woods, killed the snake, and hung it, as the keeper stated, "up to dry."

During the whole of the visit, the youth was

in an agony lest his lordship should make any allusion to their previous meeting; but the man of the world had sense and tact, and said nothing on the subject till Lawrence was walking down the private road to open the gates for him.

Then—"It is a long time since you thought to bribe me," he remarked. "I suppose you have other things to do now, besides shoot at pheasants?"

"I wish I had," answered Lawrence, in so desponding a tone that the nobleman was astonished. "I wish my father would let me go to London to push my fortune."

"Like Whittington," suggested Lord Lallard; but then, seeing his companion looked annoyed, he went on—"But why to London, and what should you do if you were there? Have you any friends—anyone who could give you a helping hand? London is a great place, and country people are apt to get lost in it."

"I do not think I should," was the answer.

"Can no situation be got for you? would a place under government——" began his lordship; but then he hesitated, and Lawrence took up his unfinished sentence for him.

"My Lord," he said, "I am not fitted for a government appointment, and it would not be fitted for me. I mean to try and push my own way in the world after my own fashion; but I thank you for your intended kindness from my heart."

It was the incident of the sovereign over again, but Lord Lallard felt that in this, as in the former instance, Lawrence was quite right.

"I have an impression," he said, "that you ought to go to London, and that you will make your fortune. Whenever you do adventure into the great Babylon, come and see me; I should like to know how you are getting on," and he held out his hand to the youth, who, leaning over the gate, watched the great man riding away towards Lallard Park, till a turn in the road hid him from sight.

That visit had been a grand event in Lawrence's life. Looking back over his old existence from the new world of Distaff Yard, the young man found himself giving much prominence, in the mental picture of his past experience he sometimes amused himself with painting, to Lord Lallard, and Lord Lallard's sorrel horse.

In the past he had suffered many minor humiliations; patched shoes, threadbare clothes, the scornful looks of the newly rich, the compassionate regards of old friends, these things were branded on his memory in letters of bitterness.

The improvements at Mallingford End, the grand carriages that came forth drawn by sleek horses out of its gates, the girl who could not ride, but yet who sallied out each day arrayed in the most perfect of habits, and tried at the very peril of her life to learn how to sit her horse; the pompous father who occupied the Mallingford pew at church, and took the lead in the responses, and gave largely at collections, and subscribed to the schools; the guests who stayed at Mallingford End in the summer, and surveyed Lawrence's thick shoes and unfashionable garments through eye-glasses, all these men and women, my hero hated with a hatred born of pride, jealousy, a consciousness of mental superiority, and a strong feeling of his own social inferiority.

He had been reared in a hard school, in one almost Spartan in its absence of all luxury or bodily indulgence, and terrible to any one possessed of the slightest sensitiveness on account of its continual humiliations.

Work, any work! to such a man after such a lot was happiness, the smallest recreation was pleasure. He ate no bread of idleness; he earned every holiday he took. He loved London—loved it as those only who have grown thoroughly sick and weary of the country ever can come to love the mighty city.

He could afford to dress better; but if he had not been able to do so, what did it matter? He was one of a crowd in the streets, and the passers by cared nothing for him, or the cut of his coat, or the make of his boots. If London be the place for the rich, it is no less the heaven of the poor. Babylon holds no second sting for those who have fallen from their once proud position into the ranks. The men composing the great army encamped there have something better to do than criticise their neighbour's looks, or meddle with his antecedents.

There is a delight in losing all sense of personal identity which can never be thoroughly appreciated till one has lived in the heart of a vast town, surrounded by busy men, and occupied women.

This delight Lawrence Barbour soon began to experience, and, as I have said, he felt happy accordingly.

From morning till night he was busy in the factory, weighing, superintending, and seeing to the packing of the goods that had to be sent out.

He became interested in fresh orders; new customers were pleasing in his eyes; he soon learned his way about London, and paid money

into banks, and collected accounts—being no
way backward in urging the necessity for immediate settlements on dilatory debtors.

In the evenings he often went over to Stepney
Causeway, and studied chemistry under Mr.
Sondes, becoming learned in alkalis and acids,
in crystals and gases, in vegetable and mineral
products, in analysis and synthesis, while Olivine
sat on a footstool beside the fire and hemmed
handkerchiefs slowly, and put in wonderfully neat
stitches.

He was a young man after Mr. Sondes' own
heart, and Mr. Perkins, thinking the matter over
to himself, decided that he ought to have been a
young man after his heart too.

What manager would ever have laboured
as Lawrence did? What hired servant could
have been trusted as he trusted this distant
kinsman?

In his time, in his work, in money matters,
the young man was unexceptionable, and yet still
Mr. Perkins felt there was something lying
between Lawrence and himself. On occasions,

he and the stranger who ate with him, worked with him, slept under his roof, came near together as acetic acid and lead; but the next moment it seemed to the chemist that nature had somehow dropped vitriol into the combination and separated the chemical product.

"I cannot make out what it is," Mr. Perkins pondered and pondered; and the more he perplexed himself about the matter, the less he understood it.

He could detect the presence of barytes in white lead; he could ferret out sulphate of soda if mixed with carbonate of soda; he could trace precipitated sulphate of lime in quinine, and tell to a grain how much potash there was in iodide of potassium; but a human analysis was quite a different matter.

Mr. Perkins happened not to be so well skilled in psychology as in chemistry; for which reason he did not know the repulsive force that prevented himself and Lawrence drawing near to one another was—selfishness.

The stranger in a strange place was labouring, not for Josiah Perkins, but for Lawrence Barbour; not for love, or gratitude, or duty, so much as for wealth, for position, and for personal success.

CHAPTER VIII.

IN THE PARK.

ALTHOUGH Mr. Perkins did not entertain the most lively affection for his kinsman, still he and Lawrence got on better than many relations who are professedly warmly attached to one another. If a man does well for himself he is pretty nearly sure to do well for his employers. There are erratic individuals, certainly, who, thinking to achieve great things for themselves, are continually leaving the irons of their masters to cool, while they thrust surreptitious irons into small fires of their own making. But these are speculative, not working men. They are people who, if started in a good trade on their own separate account to-morrow, would want to add another good trade to their former one before a week had passed.

They think a fortune is to be made in a minute; they imagine a person can do twenty different things well at once. They fancy they have "heads for organization," and such administrative minds, that they could so arrange their forces as to keep a hundred pots boiling at the same moment. They are always hopeful about new ventures; they are eternally striking out something at a "white heat," as they put it; they would like to be appointed chairmen of railway boards, chancellors of the exchequer, prime ministers—solely for the benefit of society, as they have an idea everything in creation only wants a little of their management to set it straight.

They have a contempt for their plodding neighbours. They wonder to see fortunes amassed by sheer dint of industry: if masters, they are for ever casting about to see whether a fresh experiment would not pay; if clerks, they have little speculations of their own, and are continually trying to better themselves; the consequence of all of which is, that they rarely do

well for their families, and never for their
employers.

Lawrence Barbour was not, however, one of
these. Heart and soul he flung himself into
the business at Distaff Yard; learning the ins
and outs of adulteration thoroughly and rapidly.
He was everywhere at once; the men never
knew when they were secure from him; he
seemed, young as he was, to know by intuition
who were the skulkers, the eye-servants, the
schemers, and the disaffected. He appeared and
re-appeared when and where least expected; he
never loitered on his errands; he never seemed
wearied; never grumbled at any work which
was put upon him, and withal he was uniformly
pleasant and cheerful in the house.

"Quite a treasure," Mrs. Perkins informed
her friend Mrs. Jackson, wife of the soap-boiler
in John Street. "I declare to you, ma'am, he
can match a ribbon, and remember to call at the
fishmonger's, and get a pin put in my brooch as
well or better than I can myself; I must bring
him over to tea with me some evening for you to

see," which Mrs. Perkins did, and Mrs. Jackson was charmed accordingly.

Altogether, Lawrence Barbour's start in London life was a success. He made no enemies, he gained some friends; he went oftener to the theatres perhaps than Mr. Perkins quite approved, but as he was always up and out at work the next morning by six o'clock, the chemist felt it would be ungracious for him to make any remark. Certainly also he did not take to the children; he never snubbed them, it is true, but he managed by some means to keep even Miss Ada at arm's length; and had his behaviour towards Mrs. Perkins not been of the most deferential and respectful description, it is more than likely that lady might have found fault with a young gentleman who neither nursed the "baby," aged two years, nor romped with her eldest daughter, nor made much of any member of the juvenile fry.

As it was, however, a young man who handed chairs, poured water out of the kettle, opened the door for, and never took precedence of her, who carried her prayer-book to church, and gave her his arm as they walked along the narrow street leading to St. Ann's, was not to be lightly regarded, nor wilfully quarrelled with.

Not even when Mr. Perkins was "keeping company with her," had that individual paid her such delicate attentions as Lawrence now tendered in the course of their every-day life. "He was quite chivalrous"—Mrs. Perkins pronounced the word "chevalrouse"—"in his manner," the lady was wont to declare, "and you know, Mrs. Jackson, that is a very oncommon quality in a young gentleman."

"In a young or an old, I should say," amended the soap-boiler's wife, with a sigh. "I might stand a long time before Samuel would think of offering a chair to me; and I might spend my life-time before a door, with my hands full too, without him ever stretching out a finger to open it for me. All I'd be afraid of is that a young man so polite as Mr. Barbour won't stay long in Limehouse."

"He does not seem to want to move, or, for

hat matter, indeed, to go much about London,' Mrs. Perkins replied. "He has been with us now three months, and never yet seen Hyde Park. I tell him he ought to go up and pick out one of the nice young ladies in the Row; but he only laughs, and makes a jest about there being time enough before him for that."

"He'll marry a fortune, I have no manner of doubt," said Mrs. Jackson, oracularly; whereupon Mrs. Perkins bridled up a little, and said she was sure he would marry whoever "his 'art inclined him to."

"That's just what I am saying," answered the other; "the hearts of those nice young men always do incline them to look after money."

After which speech perhaps Mrs. Perkins for a time did not like Mrs. Jackson quite so well as formerly, or treat her to so many anecdotes illustrative of Lawrence's gentlemanly behaviour. Mrs. Perkins had dreamed a dream concerning the marriage of the model young man to Ada the light-haired, and she consequently did not like to hear the probability suggested of his flying at higher game.

"There's that little Sondes," was Mrs. Jackson's parting shot. "If he can do no better, likely as not he'll marry her. Me and Mr. Jackson met the whole party of them down at Grays last Sunday, walking along the road beyond the village, as demure and pleasant as you please. Missy had on the loveliest silk you ever saw on a child's back. I should not have minded having a couple of lengths of it for gowns apiece to myself and Sophy, and——"

"'There we go,' says Mr. J. to me; 'that'll be a match some day, Mattie, mark my words.'"

"I think Mr. Jackson ought to be ashamed of himself, talking about marrying and giving in marriage in the same breath with a child like that," exclaimed Mrs. Perkins.

"Why she is six months older than your own Ada," retorted Mrs. Jackson; "and we'll see how many years will go by before you are looking after a husband for her;" and the soap-boiler's wife added, when the door closed behind her visitor, "If you are not looking out already, ma'am, which it is my opinion you are."

From that day Mrs. Perkins began to urge Lawrence to "go up on Sundays to see the parks," or to walk as far as St. Paul's or Westminster to afternoon service. "I'm sure it can't be much variety for you, spending the whole day, from one o'clock, in Stepney Causeway; and you ought to take a little change, and see more of London."

To which Lawrence replied, that some afternoon he intended, with Mr. Perkins' leave, to make his way to Hyde Park.

"You'll see the ladies there going cantering, cantering," broke in that engaging child Ada, "and the grand duchesses in their yellow carriages. I went there with pa once, and I cried because he wouldn't get me a cream-coloured pony, with a long tail, the same as I saw a little boy riding on."

"Then you were a very naughty girl," said

Mrs. Perkins, " and Cousin Lawrence won't take you with him when he goes to see the pretty ladies riding and driving."

In which statement Mrs. Perkins proved singularly correct, for without praying for the companionship of any one of his relatives, Lawrence started off all by himself one Saturday afternoon to see the glories of the western hemisphere.

It was the very height of the season. Everybody who laid claim to being anybody was in London then, and that sight which all men should see once, dazzled and bewildered the senses of the country youth.

Such carriages, such horses, such numbers of great people collected together in so small a space! Like everything else in London, the equipages seemed countless, the wealth they represented fabulous.

The tremendously got-up footmen, the bewigged coachmen, the gorgeous hammer-cloths, the exquisitely dressed women! Now walking, now stopping—Lawrence took in the spectacle, and received it as a revelation of England's power, and rank, and riches.

There they went by—great family coaches, light open carriages, dainty phaetons, broughams, containing young girls, fair matrons, old dowagers, all with the stamp of money upon them. They had been born in affluence, and brought up in ease; there was about most of them that air of calm repose, of well-bred indifference which Lawrence came thoroughly to comprehend the meaning of, in time.

Amongst the multitude, there were, indeed, many who had neither been born in the purple nor rocked in silver cradles; but the majority of the people who drove by had never known what it was to work or be poor all their lives: their existence was one continual chase after pleasure—their labour was how to enjoy themselves most—their very cares were not the cares of the commonalty. Life seemed quite another matter to them to what it did to the men and the women who regarded the grand equipages filled with fine purple merely as a very brilliant spectacle : death itself came to them delicately, over Turkey carpets, over velvet pile, through softly-closing doors, along corridors where no footfall sounded, into rooms replete with every luxury, furnished with every article, provided with every comfort which the human heart could imagine or desire.

How many times has this great show been described, and yet how rarely does any writer seem able to look at it from the plebeian side ?

The girls who blushingly recognise a favoured lover, the neglected wives who would seem, for no conceivable reason, to go out to air their misery and their riches and their discontent in the parks, the heartless countesses, the handsome roués, the men who from the footpath receive smiling salutations from the occupants of magnificent equipages, are drawn over and over and over again, while the mere ordinary observers—the mass of the spectators— are never deemed worthy of a word.

Is it that the millions are outside the pale

of civilisation, that there is no room for even a thought of them in that heaven where the Upper Ten Thousand dwell? Is it that there is such an intense pleasure in driving round the Serpentine as to preclude the possibility of any happiness outside the ranks of the privileged few who anticipate the delights of Paradise in Hyde Park?

Am I tedious? Hardly so, let me hope, since my hero stood without the charmed circle, an interested but not an envious spectator. The drive was to him but as any other show, and he paused often, and looked at it intently accordingly.

"A fine sight," said some one close beside him, and turning, he found himself face to face with a young gentleman three or four years his senior, well-dressed, good-looking, pleasant-voiced, and easy-mannered; "your first view of it, I conclude?" And, as he finished, he fixed his eyes on Lawrence's face with a stare which seemed to the latter decidedly impertinent.

"Yes, it is my first view," was the reply.

"And what do you think of it all? of the chariots and horses, of the great Mammon procession, of the vestals who are all vowed to love none other god but one, of the ancient worshippers, of the grey-haired priests? It is something to see such a show, and to be able to look upon it merely as a spectacle."

The speaker stood, leaning with his back against a tree, his arms folded, and uttered the foregoing sentence while he surveyed the carriages and their owners with a look of immeasurable superiority.

There was something in the look which nettled Lawrence's temper, and induced him to make a reply relative to sour grapes, that caused the other to laugh when he heard it.

"When a man talks about the world's prizes not being worth the having, people are apt to suspect he has failed in securing them," went on Lawrence, a little warmly.

"Answering you with your own argument, I may conclude fortune has been kinder to you than the jade has proved to me," retorted the other, with a swift look over Lawrence's attire, which made the youth feel inclined to strike him.

"I cannot understand why you should conclude anything about me at all," was the curt reply; and Lawrence walked slowly off, followed, however, by the stranger, who answered,—

" Because I have an impression I have seen you somewhere before."

"I am confident your impression is wrong, then," retorted Lawrence, and he quickened his pace.

" You mean to see everything which is to be seen—the whole performance from beginning to end ?" went on his persecutor, still keeping beside him. " Can you not recollect where we have met? for I am satisfied your face is familiar to me."

At this Lawrence stopped.

" I never saw you before," he retorted ; "and I never wish to see you again."

With which civil speech he was turning away,

when a young lady on horseback, who bowed to his companion, arrested his intention.

"You know her?" he said, addressing the stranger.

"I have that honour. Do you?"

"No I don't, but I know who she is: her father owns a place in the country which once belonged to my father."

"Then it was at Mallingford I saw you; in Mallingford Church!" exclaimed the other. "I beg your pardon; upon my honour I thought you were an old acquaintance, somebody I had known in quite another part of England. So you are Mr. Lawrence Barbour, and an even more unlucky dog than myself—Percy Forbes, at your service."

There was no resisting the stranger's voice and the stranger's manner, and Lawrence answered,—

"If I spoke rudely to you a few minutes since, I am sorry for having done so."

"And I am still more sorry for having forced my company on a comparative stranger; but since we have crossed swords and fought out our duel fairly, shall we shake hands and improve our acquaintance? I remember at Mallingford often wishing to know you; and now that chance has thrown us together, I begin to believe my wish may be gratified."

"I cannot agree with you there," Lawrence replied. "I have come to London to work, and——"

"Workers and idlers cannot long travel the same road, is that it?" was the reply. "Let us try, at any rate. Come and see me, or let me call on you," and Mr. Forbes was in the act of pulling out a card, when a great noise and tumult behind caused both men to turn sharply round. It was a horse running away.

"And a lady on him, by Jove!" exclaimed Mr. Forbes. "What the deuce are you going to do?" But without stopping to answer, Lawrence leaped over into the drive, where coachmen were drawing aside their carriages, and ladies were screaming, and men shouting.

On came the runaway. In the distance Lawrence could see the groom galloping like a madman after his mistress. There was Piccadilly before the rider — Piccadilly, and most probably death, for if she had ever possessed any control over her horse, she had lost it now.

The bridle hung loose, and she, griping the crutch of her saddle, was holding on for bare life; her hat had blown off; she had dropped her whip; her face was as white as that of a corpse; her long black hair was streaming down her back. All this Lawrence saw at the time and remembered afterwards; he felt the sunbeams dazzle him, he beheld the long line of carriages, the heads turned back to look, the footmen running after the girl, the horror-stricken faces of the bystanders; just with one glance he took all in, and the next moment he and horse and rider were lying in a confused heap in the middle of the drive.

As he caught the bridle his foot slipped. He never knew how that happened, and no one else, of course, was able to tell. When he went down, the horse fell over him, and rolling a little to the off-side saved the girl from injury.

What a crowd there was in a moment! What numbers of eager hands carried Miss Alwyn to a carriage which was at once placed at her disposal! What a sudden silence fell on all present when Lawrence was lifted from the ground, with the health on which he had piqued himself destroyed; with the strength that he had intended to use to such good purpose in winning wealth and position turned into weakness from that day forth for ever.

CHAPTER IX.

MR. SONDES' VISITOR.

It is a hard thing for a wealthy man to be struck down suddenly from strength to weakness; and when my lord gets the fingers blown off his hand, or loses the sight of one of his eyes, or is thrown in hunting, and crippled to the extent of never being able to waltz again, the world is lavish enough of its sympathy and commiseration.

"Blessed in every other respect, it is so sad," society says; and society never forgets his lamentable case, but speaks of the man softly and in whispers, and throws a certain romance over him, and compassionates the accident which has injured his health, or impaired his good looks, or prevents his killing the partridges, or bearing away the brush, with much kindness and persistency.

No one can say the world is backward about tendering its condolences on such an occasion : neither is it at all apt to forget the sufferer.

Poor Lord Adonis, and poor Sir Charles Stalwart, and poor Mr. Millionaire, and that dear deformed boy, the Earl of Mammon's son ! are these people not pitied ?   Are the sad afflictions with which, in the course of a mysterious Providence, they have been visited not talked of with lengthened faces, with lowered voices, with many shakes of the head, with many wise saws about there being troubles in all households ?

And why should they not, you ask ? Why not, indeed !   It is very sad, it is very pitiful ; it is, God knows, oftentimes very terrible, to see the wreck of a body which still, as that true woman said of her lover, suffices to hold a man's soul ; but yet—yet—oh ! friends, are we not all one flesh and blood, and is it not as hard for one human being to be maimed and lacerated, and probed and crippled, as another ?   Is it not even harder for the worker than for the man of leisure? Is it not worse for those to be sick who have to go out in the driving sleet, in the pelting rain, than for the gentlefolks who can lie in bed or sit at home in easy-chairs with cushions to their backs, with eau-de-cologne to their heads? And is it not, in conclusion, and to bring the argument up to the desired point, worse for a person to feel he will have to fight the battle of life wounded, than for his neighbour to remember that he will be for ever able to nurse his ailments by his own fireside?

The world is not tender to its workers; fortunately perhaps for them; because no man ever works so well as he who—thrusting his fist in the face of the world, denouncing its shams, cursing its hypocrisy, despising its soft words, spurning its contemptuous patronage, rejecting its insufficient help—strips himself for the conflict, trusting in nothing save the assistance of his Maker, and the strength of his own right arm.

Still, whether fortunately or unfortunately, the world is not tender towards its workers; it loads the lame man who can drive through life in his carriage with the most lavish sympathy; but how about the lame man who has to walk through existence, and earn just enough to keep himself off the parish by the way!

How! Are there not queen bees as well as drones? And what are the lives of twenty drones when compared to the comfort and well-being of one queen bee?

The world's sympathy after all is necessarily limited to the ailments and accidents of the mighty few. Too many of the rank and file are cut down every day for any strict social account to be kept of their sufferings. When the blood-horse breaks his leg, or sprains his fetlock, great is the cry of compassion; and grooms and ostlers, and trainers and owners, make lamentation over him, touching him with tender and gentle hands the while. But when his brother, the hack, falls and cuts his knees, how different! He is lashed to his feet again with many curses; trembling and shaken, he is whipped on, over the stones. There are no thousands hanging to his life ; there is nothing interesting about the poor brute ; and he is dealt with accordingly.

Behold the application—carriages, sympathy, earnest inquiries for the young lady who was not hurt,—for the young lady, who, had she been hurt, was daughter to so rich a father that every luxury would still have been at her command ; while, for the worker, a lift to the nearest hospital —in which he found himself, when he " came to," a long time afterwards.

There was one man, however, who did not follow the multitude in their laudable desire to learn how it fared with Miss Alwyn, but who rather stood to Lawrence in his distress.

He wanted, when once he heard the surgeon's opinion of the case, to have the youth removed to his own lodgings ; but the doctors so strongly recommended him to let his friend stay where he was, that Mr. Forbes bowed his will to their opinion. He wanted, however, to know if he could be of use to Lawrence, if he had any relations to whom he would wish a message con-veyed ; if there were any one he particularly desired to see; and, when it was getting quite late in the day, when Lawrence had suffered torments, and fainted during the torture many times, when all that could be done had been done, and the youth was lying "comfortably," as the nurses said, his new friend was permitted to go into the accident ward, and speak to him.

Lawrence's eyes were dim with pain and weakness, but he recognised Mr. Forbes's face in a moment, and said in a voice so low that the other had to stoop to catch his words:

"I wonder if you are my evil fate?"

"I hope not," was the reply; "what can have put such an idea into your mind?"

"Because," and the faint voice waved and shook a little, "from the moment we first met, I wanted to be rid of you—because—it was while talking to you I chanced just to catch the horse when I did. When you first spoke to me—I was strong as you are—but I shall never be sound and strong again."

He spoke all this at intervals, drawing his breath painfully and with much difficulty—with so much difficulty, indeed, that the house-surgeon came up beside him as he talked, and so chanced to catch the last part of his sentence.

"Do not say that," he remarked, before Mr. Forbes could make any answer; "we will put you to rights in a few weeks, and send you home as well as ever you were in your life."

Whereupon Lawrence turned his head towards the speaker, and gasped out, while a look of fierce despair came into his dark eyes,—

"Do you think I am a fool?—do you take me for an idiot?—do you imagine—I do not—know—that—though—if my arm—or leg—were smashed—you—might cut it off—and leave the rest of my body hale and hearty——yet what has happened to me now—it is beyond the power of your skill—or—the skill of any man—to——"

"Now I tell you what," interrupted the surgeon; "you must not talk: you must keep yourself quiet."

But Lawrence hitched his head up a little on the pillow, and drawing his breath with a sort of spasm went on:

"I may not have your knowledge—but—I have my own feelings. Do you—understand how the brute came down upon me—with its—knees doubled up. I'll be bound there was not a hair—of—the devil hurt. I can feel him now." And without any more to do, the patient closed his eyes, turned a shade whiter, if that were possible, and almost fainted as he lay. While the surgeon applied restoratives, Mr. Forbes whispered,—

"Is he speaking the truth?" To which the other answered, "Yes."

There are some patients whom it is useless to try to flatter with vain hopes; and from that time forth there was no disguise attempted towards the country lad who had come up to London to push his fortune.

He might be patched up again and pass, to ordinary observers, as sound enough; but the doctors knew, and he knew, that when the horse crashed down upon his chest, the strong vigorous health was crushed out of him for life.

Lawrence was right. With a leg broken—

with an arm gone—with far more frightful injuries to look at, the result would not have proved so disastrous; and when he awoke to full consciousness again, he would have resumed his story and taken up his parable once more; but the surgeon stopped him, remarking if he had any message he wished conveyed to his friends, Mr. Forbes might wait and receive it, but otherwise that gentleman had better go.

As Lawrence made no answer to this observation, Mr. Forbes leaned over and asked him if he had any relatives in London.

" Yes."

" You would like them of course to know where you are, and how it happened ? "

" Yes."

" If you tell me where they live I will go to them at once."

There was a pause, during the continuance of which Lawrence seemed to be fighting a battle with his lungs for breath. Mr. Forbes was going to speak again, when the other suddenly broke out :—

"I do not want you to trouble yourself about me; I did not stop *your* horse; I did not save *your* life, and unless you are in love with the girl, I cannot see any claim——"

"I never said you had any claim," interrupted Mr. Forbes, quietly enough, though he coloured to his very temples either with vexation or anger; "but you cannot help my giving you my admiration for as brave and rash an action as I ever saw performed. You cannot hinder my being your friend, whether you choose to be mine or not."

"There must be an end of this, gentlemen," remarked the surgeon. "Mr. Forbes, I am sorry to have to seem hard, but you really cannot remain here any longer."

"Tell me where I am to go," entreated Percy, laying a persuasive hand on Lawrence's, which was stretched out over the coverlid; "if you do not wish me to do anything for you in the future, at all events let me be of some little service to you in the present. I am not one of the Alwyns; I did not buy Mallingford; I am not a rich man:

I am a struggling one like yourself, and I only want to do for you now what I hope some other man would do for me, if I were lying here in your place. Tell me where your friends live," and there came such a pleading tone into his voice, such an eager, earnest expression into his face, that Lawrence, almost in spite of himself as it seemed, was forced to answer:

"Go to Mr. Sondes. He lives in Stepney Causeway, Commercial Road, and tell him Lawrence Barbour, who is lying here with his breast-bone broken and every rib dislocated, would like——"

"He can see you to-morrow," interposed the surgeon, answering his questioning look.

"Commercial Road, where?" asked Mr. Forbes.

"Limehouse," was the reply; "beg him—to tell—Mr. Perkins," added Lawrence, who was inwardly anathematising his own cowardice in not allowing this fashionably-dressed young fellow, who seemed so grievously in want of employment, to go due East to Distaff Yard.

But he could not do it. He had not moral courage enough at that moment to bid Mr. Forbes encounter Mrs. Perkins and the children, and the vulgarity of the small common establishment.

Even in health he would have had to put all pride in his pocket before introducing any stranger to such a family circle as that; and now in sickness, with a dreadful depression weighing him down, with every word a pain to utter, with every breath he drew hurting him, with a terrible faint sickness coming continually over him, he was quite unable even to contemplate such a visit calmly, and so compromised matters with his own conscience by telling it Mr. Sondes' house was nearer and easier to find than Distaff Yard.

"Anything else?" asked Mr. Forbes, before he departed.

"Yes—one moment—if there is any danger, he might write to my father."

"There is no danger," said the surgeon. "There is not," he repeated, seeing Lawrence's eyes were fastened doubtfully on his face.

"Then Mr. Sondes had better see you before writing to your father," suggested Mr. Forbes. "Now, good-by. Keep up your spirits. I'll call and see how you are to-morrow," and the young man turned and left the ward accompanied by the surgeon, who having taken an amazing fancy, not to his patient, but to his patient's friend, walked with the latter as far as the outer door.

"A singular youth," he remarked. "May I ask if you have known him long?"

"No; but I have long known who he is—a son of Mr. Barbour, who was formerly owner of Mallingford End; and the young lady whose horse he stopped to-day is Miss Alwyn, daughter of Mr. Alwyn, of Hereford Street *and* Mallingford End, Hertfordshire."

"Bless my soul! how singular! quite romantic!" In a moment, and without tedious explanations, the surgeon recognised the peculiarity of the position. Clearly his brains did not require to be poked after and stirred up into action like the very inefficient brains of many people. "It is a hard case," he went on. "Is Mr. Barbour—our young friend, I mean—pos·sessed of an independent income?"

"On the contrary: he has lately come to London in order to engage in business."

"He had better go back to the country," was the reply. "His chest will never stand desk work again."

"Miss Alwyn ought, in my opinion, to marry him," said Percy Forbes. "It is the least she can do, I think, under the circumstances," and a smile, which certainly was not quite pleasant, curled the young man's lips as he propounded this idea. "It is a great pity we did not take him to Hereford Street and let her nurse him through it;" and Percy laughed outright this time, while the surgeon said, inquiringly, "She was not hurt?"

"Hurt; not in the least. He got the whole benefit of the accident."

"A good horsewoman?" But Percy did not answer. He only shook hands with the surgeon and laughed again, before he went away along

Piccadilly and hailed a cab, and bade the driver take him as fast as he could to Stepney Causeway.

It was late in the evening before he reached the old house; but he found Mr. Sondes still seated in the dining-room with his wine untasted before him. Lawrence had promised to call on his way back from the West, and Mr. Sondes was waiting for his appearance when Mr. Forbes entered.

"I have a message for you," the gentleman stated, after the first commonplaces were over, "from a relative of yours, if I am not mistaken, —Mr. Lawrence Barbour."

"He is not my relative," answered Mr. Sondes; "but that is of no consequence. What is the message? Has the lad been getting himself into any mess?"

"He has met with an accident," answered Mr. Forbes. "He will not be able to come home to-night, nor for many nights, I fear;" and without any further preface or hesitation, he went on to tell Mr. Sondes all about his meeting with

Lawrence, about the runaway horse, about the accident.

Across these details, however, Mr. Sondes cut relentlessly.

"Is he badly hurt?" he asked. "Tell me the worst, sir, I beg. Is he in danger? I am no relation. Do not be afraid to speak."

"He is in no danger; but he is very badly hurt—so badly that I do not think he can ever be very strong again. He is sadly injured about the chest."

"And he has his way to make in the world!"

"That is the worst part of the business," said Mr. Forbes. "He will never be able to sit at a desk again."

"He never has sat at a desk," retorted Mr. Sondes. "He never is likely to have to sit at one: and if it comes to that, what do you know about desks, sir? You do not look as if you and work of any kind were very intimate acquaintances."

"Poverty makes people acquainted with strange bed-fellows," retorted Mr. Forbes. "Business and I know more of each other than you might imagine. Is there anything I can do for you at the West?" he added, rising, and holding his hat so gracefully the while, that Mr. Sondes thought him a fop, and disliked him accordingly.

Still, common politeness demanded that he should ask this man, who had taken such trouble in Lawrence's behalf, to remain and have wine, or coffee, or dinner, or something; and accordingly Mr. Sondes did press his hospitality on Percy Forbes much more earnestly than was his wont.

But nothing could induce his visitor to prolong his stay. "I have an engagement this evening I must keep," he said, and he moved towards the door, Mr. Sondes following.

"I will walk with you till you get a cab," said that gentleman, who felt perhaps that his best manner seemed a little rough to this individual, who affected the hours, and fashions, and habits of the West. "The Commercial Road is not the pleasantest street in the world for a stranger to find his way along."

They were by this time standing together in the hall, and while Mr. Sondes was looking about for his hat, Percy Forbes remarked on the beauty of the garden, which he could see through that doorway which now leads out into the wretchedest of wretched yards.

There were a few steps down from the hall to the doorway, and at the foot of the steps, framed in the dark oak, and with the green of the grass-plot, and the bright flowers in the garden for background, stood Olivine, looking half-shyly half-curiously at the stranger.

"Your little daughter?" said Mr. Forbes, inquiringly.

"No, my niece.—Olivine, come here."

Obediently, but still slowly, she ascended the short flight of stairs. She came out of the light of the summer's evening into the dark hall, and still nestling a kitten to her heart, offered her hand at her uncle's desire to the strange gentleman.

As she did so she lifted her eyes to his face, which was frank and fearless, and handsome enough to win a child's admiration and affection.

He stroked the kitten, and he stroked her hair; then he said, looking in the sweet pensive little face, " Will you kiss me, dear ?"

Without the least hesitation she put her lips to his, and kissed him as he asked her; then he bade her good-by, and walked out into the street, accompanied by her uncle, and—forgot her!

He did not imagine then, there would ever come a time when at thought of that girl his manhood would fail him—his courage and determination fade away. He could not tell then that when the years had gone by, at the very sight of Olivine his heart would be moved, and his spirit shaken like a reed; that she would grow to be more to him than any human being had ever been before, or might ever be again; that he would tremble at the touch of her hand, and change colour at the sound of her voice.

He could not foresee, as he paced slowly down

Stepney Causeway and into the Commercial Road, how the events of that day were destined to be wound in and out through every year of his future life; how they were to appear and reappear in the web of his existence, forming strange and unexpected patterns, and weaving in threads now dark, now light, as the spinning went on from day to day, and from month to month, till the work was completed, and the tale told.

See him, as he walks along, with his thick chestnut hair stirred by the evening breeze, with his brownish-grey eyes looking to right and left at the strange people and the strange place in which he found himself. See this man, whose life had been so different to Lawrence's, glancing at the locality in which my hero's lot was cast; see him, and stamp his features on your memory, for he has almost as much to do with this story as Lawrence Barbour himself.

Tall and handsome, and distinguished-looking, with waving chestnut hair, a broad square fore-head, a frank kindly mouth, eyes of that wonderful brown-grey, as I have said, trim whiskers, and closely-shaven chin.

There was, however, something foppish about him; something, perhaps, a little effeminate and provoking; something almost too cool and self-possessed in his manners. Life did not appear to be life in very earnest to him. He had none of Lawrence Barbour's fierce energy and defiant resolution.

He had been brought up in a different school, and he entered that school with a different nature; yet the two never wholly lost sight of one another from that day, when, after separating from Mr. Sondes, Percy Forbes drove straight to his lodgings, arrayed himself in evening costume, and then went off to Hereford Street, where he was received by both Mr. and Miss Alwyn with, figuratively speaking, open arms.

CHAPTER X.

In an essay of Pope's addressed to Sir Richard
Temple, the poet alludes to the owner of a house
that stood at the corner of Grosvenor Place, in
lines which I quote, although they may seem for
the moment to have no connection with St.
George's Hospital, where Lawrence Barbour lay
through the lovely summer weather, lamenting
his ill-fortune, chafing over the accident that
kept him still a prisoner.

Speaking of the " ruling passion," Pope
says :—

> " Old politicians chew on wisdom past,
> And totter on in business to the last ;
> As weak, as earnest, and as gravely out,
> As sober Lauesborough dancing in the gout."

This was the Lord Lanesborough who more than an hundred and fifty years ago sought an interview with Queen Anne, and advised her Majesty to dissipate her grief for the loss of her husband—by dancing !

This was the Lord Lanesborough who stated, on the front of his house for the information of all passers by :—

> " It is my delight to be
> Both in town and country."

This was the Lord Lanesborough who lived and danced in that mansion which formerly occupied the ground now covered by St. George's Hospital. Changes seem occasionally to have been effected almost as rapidly in former days as in our times. Queen Anne only ascended the throne in 1702, and his lordship must have kept his residence for many a long day after that, just beyond the " Turnpike House." Yet, in 1733, St. George's was completed, being opened for the reception of patients on New Year's Day, 1734.

Opposite to the site which the hospital now

occupies there was formerly one of the numerous forts which were raised by the inhabitants of London in 1642, when fears were entertained of an attack by the Royal army.

Looking at the old maps, the ancient turnpike house, which we must take as our standing point, would seem to have been perfectly in the country at the time Lord Lanesborough resided opposite Hide Park, as it was spelt in those days.

So late indeed as 1770 the hospital appears to have been entirely surrounded by country. Literally it stood in the parish of St. George's in the Fields.

Tattersall's did not begin its existence until nine years afterwards. Grosvenor Place also had still to be built, as well as Chapel and Halkin Streets, the whole of Belgravia, and Pimlico. Indeed it is only about thirty years since the Five Fields, " where robbers lie in wait," was broken up into building ground. What changes the old hospital has seen, and what changes still remain for it to see!

Tattersall's life began when St. George's had

attained a respectable age, and Tattersall's is now gone; Grosvenor Place is going. Will there ever be a railway through St. George's and Rotten Row, or is that the point at which British endurance would rebel?

Still we are living now at such a pace that actually the things which are here to-day, are away to-morrow.

We let a week slip by without passing through some familiar thoroughfare, and when we enter it again, behold the old place seems strange to us! How, therefore, will it fare before many years have passed with St. George's, out of which I would paint an interior, on which the summer sun shone brightly?

It was a cheerful room, with many windows, light and well ventilated. There were the inevitable rows of beds; there were the pale faces of the haggard, the aged, the weary, resting on the pillows in every variety of position. There were the flowers, growing as flowers belonging directly or indirectly to the poor always do grow, luxuriantly,—in pots placed in front of the

window at the extreme end of the ward. There were
men convalescent sitting up, and driving those who
were grievously sick and distressed in body and
mind almost out of their senses at sight of their
robuster health; there were boys, little boys,
leaning over the sides of their beds and playing
with simple toys, as you, reader, have seen, or
may see them doing at this present hour.
There was the same wonderful silence, the same
absence of complaint, as strikes a stranger
entering any London hospital for the first time;
further, there was the same cleanliness, the same
order, the same absence of everything calculated
to produce nausea or horror, as is the case in
this year of grace in which I am writing.

There was sickness, which is incident to
humanity; there was sorrow, which it is the
will of God shall fall to the lot of many; there
was suffering, which skill can oftentimes merely
palliate, not cure: but there was charity, there
was help, there was constant care.

All man's efforts, we know, are incapable of
perfection. His finest charities are liable to

abuse, his best-conceived schemes fall short of the mark, his most holy intentions get soiled with the dust and dirt of our mortality, and there is no work that he can execute in which faults may not be detected; but still, what man could do, had been done here. Even Lawrence Barbour, who anathematised the students, and employed himself in spying out the nakedness of the land, admitted that, as a whole, the place was well managed, and said he did not think he could have been better taken care of had he been a peer of the realm.

He made this statement to Mr. Sondes, lying, not in the accident ward, to which shortly after his entrance there chanced to come a great accession of patients, but occupying a bed in one of the upstairs wards, where visitors not a few were wont to gather round him.

He was getting slowly better, but the terrible depression which usually follows such injuries as he had received could not easily be got rid of. He suffered dreadful physical pain, but that was as nothing in comparison to the mental torture which, as the days went by, increased, rather than diminished.

"What shall I be fit for?" he was asking Mr. Sondes on the day when I again take up the thread of my story. "For God's sake tell me what I shall be fit for when I leave this place!"

"Have patience, my boy; do not despair: we shall find something," replied Mr. Sondes. "By-the-by, has Mr. Alwyn been to see you?"

"Yes," answered Lawrence, "he has been here three times—twice when I was too ill to talk to any person, and once when I was allowed to see him. He came," went on Mr. Lawrence Barbour, "dressed in his everlasting light grey trousers, and his black waistcoat, and he had that watch-chain which I know so well, with seals attached to it, and his boots creaked, and he received much respect at the hands both of doctors and nurses."

"Now do not talk," entreated Mr. Sondes; "you know talking is bad for you."

"Then what on earth do you ask me questions

for ?" retorted the other. "I tell you, Mr.
Sondes, if I do not talk to some one I shall
go mad. I lie here hour after hour, think, think,
thinking. It is no child's play enduring one's
own reflections in such a place as this. Mr.
Alwyn wanted to take me to his house, but I
and the doctor jointly declined his offer. He is
in great distress. He is the grand seigneur no
more. He is going to write to my father and
press upon him the hospitalities of Hereford
Street. I lie quiet when it is getting dusk, and
consider Mr. Alwyn, and wonder where the
sugars and spices grow that produce such
fortunes."

He spoke all this at intervals, but still would
not suffer Mr. Sondes to interpose a word till
he had quite finished, when that gentleman
remarked—

"You are cynical."

"Am I? If so, it is the fault of Mr. Alwyn
and his money. I wonder if gold have a scent
—if the smell of it be carried in the air—if the
knowledge thereof groweth like the stature of a

goodly tree. I shut my eyes, and Mr. Alwyn rises to my view, Mammon incarnate; and then I consider my own almost helpless future. Oh, Lord! oh, Lord! was it not hard to deal with me thus?" And Lawrence turned his face aside, and—may I say it, without impeaching his manhood—wept.

What is there to tell about those days, spent as they were in one of London's great and useful hospitals; what is there to chronicle, save that the man (was he not one by reason of his struggle and his suffering) slept and ate and drank, and swallowed his medicine by rule and order, and had visitors when he was allowed, and thought at all times and seasons most convenient to himself.

Mr. Perkins came often to see him, arrayed in his Sunday clothes, and exhibiting the most wonderful waistcoat it had as yet entered into Lawrence's head to conceive of any person wearing as a matter of choice.

He looked, as all such persons do look when respectably dressed, excessively ill at ease, but he evidently considered his costume the correct thing for an hospital close to Hyde Park, and consoled himself for any discomfort it entailed accordingly.

On the whole, I think Lawrence liked talking to his kinsman best of all his visitors. Mr. Perkins told him about the latest dodge in coffee berries; about a recent detection of spurious nutmegs; made him his confidant concerning a method, a new method he had discovered, of coating peppercorns, and spoke cheerfully of such work as Lawrence could do whether his chest were made sound or not.

This guest was certainly more successful in winning gracious words from Lawrence than Mr. Alwyn, who was a business man, with Money written on every line, on every wrinkle, on every feature, on every fold of his attire, and yet who aped the fashionable man of solid West-End standing all the time.

He was, though not an old man, old-fashioned in his dress, address, style of living, choice of wines, and so forth; but yet, spite of all this, ill-natured people said Mr. Alwyn was not quite so antiquated in his business ideas as his tailor was in the cut of his clothes.

As to his appearance Mr. Alwyn was a heavy-looking individual of fifty, with a slight tendency towards a " corporation," who always, as Lawrence remarked, wore grey trousers, a black frock coat, a black waistcoat, a watch which he carried in a fob. Attached to this watch were various keys and seals, which jingled as Mr. Alwyn drew forth his chronometer, and checked it against the surgeon's silver turnip.

The man was, as Lawrence said, " Mammon incarnate ; and he wants me to go and stay at his house," laughed the youth, as well as he was able. " To go and stay with him, and make acquaintance with his daughter ! I told the old fellow she never had ridden, and never could ride. I told him we used to watch her coming out of the park gates at Mallingford, and prophesy that she would break her neck some day, but that I little thought it was I who should suffer from her want of skill. He looked very grave at first over it, but seems to have come to the conclusion I was right after all, and wants to improve our knowledge of one another; as if we did not know too much of each other already," and Lawrence laughed again.

Imagine such sentences as these, uttered with difficulty at intervals; fancy that conversations of this description were the only bright spots in the monotony of that weary time, and then picture to your own imagination, each reader among the number I am happy to be now addressing, what a purgatory it must have seemed to a person of Lawrence Barbour's active nature.

It would be easy to tell you of the breaks in his life, of his various visitors, of how the men from Distaff Yard came in little relays to see him, and were wont, after the manner of their fraternity, to shake hands till the patient screamed with the pain such shaking caused. There would be no difficulty in setting forth all this—in recalling out of the past the conversations that were held, the trivial circumstances which were repeated; but how should I ever find words to tell you about the interminable hours and days when he was alone, during the course of which he thought of the cruel accident that had left him stranded and disabled, like a ship-wrecked vessel, on the shores of life?

How could I ever hope to convey to you an idea of the diligence with which he cursed his destiny, of the persistency he displayed in refusing all medical comfort, in disbelieving all surgical reports?

It is not given to all men to sit down in silence, making no sign while the tempest sweeps by. There are not many who can possess their souls with patience, and if there be, such patience, was not vouchsafed at any rate to Lawrence Barbour.

He had suffered and was suffering, and he could not help repining. His health was gone, and his occupation to a great extent gone with it.

What should he be, this prematurely old young man? What was to be his lot in life? How was money still to be made?—how was the ground to be roped off—the bets booked—the race won?

True he knew the battle is not always 'to the strong, and so—for youth is very hopeful—he sometimes trusted things might yet go well with him. Upon the other hand, Lawrence's nature, though not melancholy, was yet like the natures of many energetic individuals, inelastic; further, his physical condition was depressing in the extreme, and oftener than I could tell, he got into straits of despondency which were most wearing to himself, and trying to those interested in his recovery.

All at once, however, there came a change. Mr. Barbour senior arrived in London in a much more desponding state of mind than even that in which it pleased Lawrence to revel, and wished to take his boy home with him.

At the very mention of this, Lawrence fired up.

Was it for a trumpery accident his father desired he should relinquish the hopes and plans of his life? Was his father dreaming when he demanded such a sacrifice? Did the doctors say he was fit for nothing but vegetating in the country? Then the doctors lied! He, Lawrence Barbour, meant to show the whole of them, relations, friends, foes, surgeons, what he could yet do in spite of his dislocated ribs and his unsound chest.

"Not win the race!" he muttered; "we shall see." And from that time forth he ceased complaining, he ceased fretting, and lay through the length of those tantalizingly fine summer days, planning, thinking, determining; more resolute, and more persistent, than ever as to his future course.

CHAPTER XI.

ONE OF MAMMON'S ELECT.

THERE are drawbacks to most things ; a curse oftentimes walks side by side with a blessing; there are few pleasant days in life over which no cloud comes to cast a shadow, and there is scarcely any talent that can be bestowed upon man but contains within itself some corresponding disadvantage.

To cleverness perhaps the drawback is chiefly that even cleverness must have its youth. A man or woman, as a rule, cannot be like other people through boyhood or girlhood and then suddenly bud out into genius. The tree shows early what it is going to bear, and in the human subject it is apt to develope its proclivities with rather a disagreeable amount of *empressement*.

Sweet youth! innocent youth! guileless youth! trusting youth! ingenuous youth! exclaim our poets, and rhapsodize accordingly; but it never enters into the head of even the most unpractical of writers to say there is anything charming about youth if it be clever.

Somehow cleverness is not a robe which young people ever seem able to wear with humility. It is too gorgeous for them; they go about vaunting their plumage, and setting up their splendid feathers for all the world to take note of and admire. Farther, they appear to think that the Almighty has made them a rare species by themselves, and are arrogant accordingly.

The consciousness of power is a fine thing; it carries a man through many an uneven way, over many a terrible obstacle; but till people have learned that even power is not everything, till they have had many a rub, many a fall, many a hard lesson, great mental strength and unusual talent are apt to make our acquaintances a trifle disagreeable. Even inferiority does not like to be ridden over roughshod. A donkey may have a tender mouth, and till the garments of genius lose a little of their pristine freshness, till their wearer ceases to be recognised by them instead of by himself, till he subdues his manner and walks soberly and discreetly along the highways of existence, till, in fact, the newness of being cleverer than his fellows ceases to oppress him, and to tinge his address with arrogance, it is to be feared that no one outside his own circle of intimate friends and relations will be much enchanted with the great future chemist, or doctor, or lawyer, or author, or engineer, or man of business.

True genius, we are occasionally told, is always modest and retiring; but if this be the case, true genius very rarely walks abroad, except in its extreme old age.

Fact is, perhaps, that precocity always tries to stand too high. It is never contented to remain in the plains, but is eternally striving to reach the hills, where sit the greybeards and the sages.

Essentially, the characteristic of youthful talent is mental loneliness; and mental loneliness is just one of those things with which ordinary humanity has no patience; for which it has no toleration.

Mediocrity resents it as a personal affront, inferiority regards it with awe and wonder, sympathy is flung back by it, kindness fails to melt the ice; and consequently the youth, pressing onward to distinction, pursues his way in solitude, thinking the world perhaps as hard and cold, as the world thinks him disagreeable and conceited.

The world, that portion of it I mean with which Lawrence Barbour chanced at this period of his history to be thrown in contact, arrived vaguely at some such conclusions concerning my hero as those which I have been endeavouring to set forth.

He was no favourite in hospital. Neither doctors nor nurses were greatly charmed by him.

Everything that skill could do for his ailments was done, yet Lawrence made no sign of real thankfulness.

There was, however, this much to be urged on his side of the question, that he certainly was in the position of that individual whom the Irishman was employed to flog.

"Bad cess to ye," exclaimed the Hibernian, "whether I hit high, or whether I hit low, it's all the same, nothing satisfies ye."

For precisely the same reason perhaps nothing thoroughly satisfied Lawrence. It was a bad business, and the surgeons could only make a patch-work affair of all their mending. As regarded Mr. Alwyn, it was his duty to come and inquire after the health of the man who lay enduring torments, because a young lady who did not know how to ride had been permitted to mount a spirited horse. Likewise, Lawrence felt that Miss Alwyn was merely performing a needful courtesy when she sent him rare flowers, and fruits, and kind messages, intermixed with many regrets.

He was wont to turn the flowers over somewhat contemptuously after Mr. Alwyn left, and to remark that he supposed they had been grown at Mallingford.

Further, he never touched the fruit, but let

whomsoever would, eat it with the sublimest self-denial.

He had curious ideas on many subjects, and as he never hesitated to broach his opinions if occasion arose for his doing so, he came in time to be regarded as a singular case, not merely by reason of his injury, which was exceptional, but also because of his mental organisation, which was peculiar.

For this reason, if Lawrence did not win love, he arrested attention. His powers of endurance were so great, his capacity for suffering was so extreme, the intensity of his despair so pitiful, and the courage with which he faced the worst and defied it, so rare, that whether those around liked or disliked him, they could not help being attracted by such a nature. Strength, whether for evil or for good, energy, whether of mind or of body, has a fascination for the most of us; and this young man was so strong in all those points, wherein the majority of his fellows were weak, he had such powers in him, undeveloped though they might be, there was such a conscious superiority in the way he spoke, in the answers he returned to questions, in his bearing towards Mr. Alwyn, that even the great man himself pronounced Lawrence to be a "remarkable fellow," and professed his inability to make head or tail of him.

"He is very ugly, papa, is he not?" asked Miss Alwyn, when he advanced this theory of Lawrence being an enigma.

Parent and child were seated at the time in the drawing-room of their house, in Hereford Street, and Mr. Alwyn, being rather given to renewed inspections of his premises, looked all round the apartment before he answered.

"No, not ugly, my dear; decidedly not ugly. Do you not remember seeing him at Mallingford? A plain young man, perhaps, but certainly not ugly."

"I remember him very well indeed," answered Miss Alwyn. "He used to be continually staring up at our pew in church, and I thought him hideous."

"No person could be hideous with such eyes as his, Etta," answered Mr. Alwyn.

" Why, what kind has he got ? " inquired Miss Henrietta, who knew all about Lawrence Barbour's eyes a great deal better than her father.

" They are dark, clever, piercing eyes," replied the rich man, " eyes, that never seem to be off one's face, and that go travelling down into one's thoughts, and reading them. And he does read them, too," added Mr. Alwyn, "for he has answered me time after time according to my thoughts, rather than my words. A remarkable youth : I should not wonder if he rises to eminence some of these days."

" Now, you dear old thing, don't say that, please, don't," entreated Miss Alwyn; "I am quite weary of hearing you prophesy great things about young men who never rise at all. There's Percy Forbes, papa, what was he not to be ? to what height was he not to rise, and now the handsome creature will do nothing but dance attendance on pretty girls, and is satisfied if he can earn sufficient to keep him in gloves and perfumes. Say Lawrence Barbour will not rise, and I shall believe in him, say he is not clever, and I shall expect to see a book of his reviewed in a week's time, or to hear of his being Solicitor General, or Lord Chancellor, or something equally desirable before he is thirty."

"I cannot tell what to make of him, that I cannot."

"Then do not try to make anything, but let us see what he will turn out. Is he more grateful now for your constant visits than formerly: does he seem properly impressed at the attention you pay him?"

"Etta!"

It was very rarely Mr. Alwyn ventured to rebuke his daughter, but there certainly was a sharp reproof conveyed in his tone, which Miss Alwyn feeling, coloured, and remained silent.

"I do not consider anything we can do for him too much under the circumstances," went on Mr. Alwyn. "He risked his life to save yours, and he did save it, I have no doubt, for had Firefly once turned into Piccadilly, there is no telling what fearful injuries you might not have sustained. Lord Lallard thinks precisely the same as I do. He was at the hospital to-day when I got there, chatting away to Mr. Barbour as though he were his brother, and he walked back with me as far as the Marble Arch. He was inquiring very particularly about you, Etta, and intends to call."

"I am greatly honoured," answered Miss Etta, with a mocking courtesy. "We have been his lordship's neighbours for so long, that it is delightful to think he is going to condescend to make our acquaintance at last. And so he thinks you are bound to be grateful for ever to the young man, and that you are doing nothing more than your duty in marching over to St. George's every day! I wonder if he would think the same had a groom stopped Firefly; I wonder if he would think we ought to send fruit and flowers, and all manner of things, were a crossing-sweeper lying in Lawrence Barbour's place."

And the young lady, who was getting angry, spoke harshly and scornfully as she concluded her tirade.

"We could pension off a groom,—we could

give a crossing-sweeper a sum of money——"
began Mr. Alwyn.

"I understand; and as, though the Barbours
are miserably poor, they are too proud to take
money, we are to go on for ever, I suppose, paying
attentions to the family. We shall have to ask
old Mr. Barbour to Mallingford when we go
down there, and entertain the other brother, and
beg Mr. Lawrence Barbour to consider this house
his home. In fact we are to go through life
burdened by the sense of an obligation which
we can never hope to pay off, and I shall hear
whispered at every turn, ' There is the young
gentleman who saved Miss Alwyn's life.' I wish
he had let the horse alone, I would rather have
had my legs broken, or my neck broken, for that
matter, than be compelled to carry such an in-
cubus about with me."

"The real fact is, Percy has vexed you; is it
not so?" said Mr. Alwyn. "He told us, to
begin with, or rather he told you, that Lawrence
Barbour would not come cap in hand to any
man living. You were full that first night of

what we were to do for the youth, of how we were to ask his father up to stay with us; of how he must be brought over here, and I remember well Percy remarking, 'You can ask him, of course; but I do not think you will get him to take up his abode with you, for he is as proud as Lucifer, and as independent as possible.' And when I did ask him and he refused, you grew angry, and wanted me not to go to the hospital any more. You are not right in this matter, Etta; though you are my daughter, I must say I think you are wrong."

" Well, you have said it, so let us talk no more about him. Next thing I suppose you will be wanting *me* to go to St. George's."

" Percy said you ought," mildly suggested Mr. Alwyn.

" I wish Percy Forbes and Lawrence Barbour were both sewn up in a sack and at the bottom of the Thames," retorted Miss Alwyn, and she rose as she spoke and apparently in order to put an end to the discussion went over to her piano and commenced singing.

Seated afar off, Mr. Alwyn sat and listened and beat time with his head and fingers; but his thoughts were not with the music so much as with the singer, his only child, of whom he was proud and yet afraid—whom he loved a vast deal more than she loved him.

Let me try to sketch them both for you as they were then—father and daughter; the rich man, and the solitary creature who was near and dear to him on earth.

Mr. Alwyn was one of those men who never by any chance seem to unbend. Easy chairs had no attraction for him; if by chance he selected one he did not lean back in it like anybody else, but sat rather bent forward a little, with his legs apart, and his feet firmly planted on the carpet.

No human being had ever seen Mr. Alwyn lying on a sofa, neither was it in the memory of any, even of his oldest acquaintances that they had beheld him resting with his arm upon a chimney-piece. When he stood, he stood upright, when he sat, he never stretched out his limbs, nor lolled in a chair, nor took his ease in any way.

People said Mr. Alwyn had too much money to be able to take his ease, and perhaps this assertion was correct. His money was a great trouble to Mr. Alwyn, as money always is to those who are reported to have more of it than is actually the case.

Mr. Alwyn was rich, very rich; but the world called him a millionaire, and therein the world was wrong. He had not made his money easily, he had not made it perfectly honestly. His hands were not so clean as they had been thirty years before : he had not found the ways of commerce, ways of pleasantness; and emphatically he had not found its paths those of peace.

He had not exactly risen from the ranks, he was not one of those men who, coming into London hatless and shoeless, are borne out of the great Babylon to one of the " silent cities " in a hearse with nodding plumes, amid the noise of much lamentation and weeping. On the contrary, his father had been in business before him, and his grandfather before that. He sprang from a class which finds it much harder to get on in the world than a class infinitely lower, because the members composing it are fettered in the earlier stages of their career by the opinions of the clique in which they live, and move, and have their being.

The lad who has swept out an office, and eaten without any feeling of shame, but rather with an appreciative relish, three pennyworth of beefsteak pudding, rides a light-weight in the race for wealth, against the man who has always associated respectability with rates and taxes; who believes in keeping up a certain appearance, who has many pulls on his purse and more on his temper, who regards the opinions of those about him, who considers a certain amount of furniture and a given style of dress indispensable, and who mounts the business steed, cumbered by prejudices and fears, and oppressed by much gentility.

Given two boys, with equal push and ability,

—the one the son of nobody, who keeps your crossing clean, and who, when he shuts up shop, by, as it has been neatly put, " sweeping the mud up on the pavement," goes away to sleep in some wretched lodging; and the other, the son of a man earning three, or four, or five hundred a year, shall we say; put them out in life the one as errand-boy, the other as junior-clerk : which of these has the best chance of success ?

The one is educated; the other is not;—the one is socially much higher than his fellow; the other is but, in the world's estimation, as the mud he once swept aside from his crossing;— the one has friends to help him ; the other must take his leaps for himself;—the one apparently has far the best chance; the other has, so far as can be seen, every circumstance dead against him ;—and yet, look you, the poor boy gets the lead of the race, because he is not weighted unduly; because he has been able to steal a-head, while no one was thinking of him—no one criti- cising how he rode.

The rates and the taxes, the eating and drinking, the clothing and servants, the opinions of friends, the ideas of society,—all tend to keep a man of the middle class in the valley of mediocrity all his life. He is influenced by his surroundings: his next door neighbour is a person of consequence in his eyes,—Mrs. Grundy a power which he fears to ignore.

Mrs. Grundy had, all his life, stood between Mr. Alwyn and comfort. From his youth upward, that typical female had exercised a baneful influence on his happiness, and in his latter years, when wealth and abundance had been gained, and something far and away more than competence secured, Mr. Alwyn still allowed the maxims of that disagreeable individual to influence his conduct her ideas to affect his mode of life.

Society was pleased, as I have said, to call Mr. Alwyn a millionaire, and Mr. Alwyn did not contradict society. He knew as well as anybody on earth, that if he were, as some people facetiously remarked, one of Mammon's elect, he had not as yet entered into the kingdom. He was perfectly well aware that, while the world thought he was not living up to anything like his income, it yet would have puzzled his wits greatly had anything occurred to compel him to increase his expenditure. He had visible wealth—he had a fair house in town, well and handsomely furnished—he had pictures—he had statuettes—he had men-servants and women-servants—he had Mallingford, where were gardeners, and gamekeepers, and grooms, and more men and more women—he had carriages and horses —he entertained liberally—he was not niggardly about giving to the poor and the needy.

All this he was able to do—able without running any risk, without spending a penny beyond what was justifiable to accomplish ; but the world thought, because they saw so much wealth, that the man was about twice as wealthy as happened actually to be the case.

If Mr. Alwyn ventured to hint he was not so rich as people took him to be, his assertion was received either with polite incredulity or laughed at as a capital joke. "Not wealthy, my dear fellow ? you are only *too* wealthy," was the usual reply; and Mr. Alwyn, like many others, had to bow his head beneath the weight of the crown which was forced upon him.

CHAPTER XII.

HEREFORD STREET.

THE reader who follows this story to the end will find that the young lady whom we left in the last chapter seated at her piano, plays an important part in it, and exercises a considerable influence on the fortunes and happiness of the hero.

After this statement, no apology can be considered necessary for devoting a few pages to Miss Alwyn, and the house which you will be asked many a time to enter before the " Race for Wealth " is ended, and the goal of completion reached.

There is one glory of the sun and another of the moon, and there is also one style of beauty among women which is angelic and another which is—not.

Miss Alwyn's beauty was, as Percy Forbes remarked in after days, not the beauty of an angel, nor of a woman, but of a devil.

It is painful to hear hard words used concerning a lady, and not to be able to contradict them; but what he said chanced unfortunately to be true. She was beautiful exceedingly, fascinating beyond all powers of description; and yet her beauty was not a thing to be desired or coveted. Her fascination was of that kind from which all honest men might pray God to deliver them.

There are faces that we do not take to much at first; from which instinct—so much more reliable in its warnings than sense ever is in its assurances—bids us flee; and Henrietta Alwyn's was one of these.

But still the majority of men did not flee: they turned to take another look, and were lost. For the singular eyes attracted them—the hair, which Percy said was like the coils of a snake, entangled them; her smile bewitched, her manner intoxicated them; and he who once passed through the ordeal of loving Henrietta Alwyn, never came forth from it quite scatheless —quite the same as he had been before.

She was young, too — only one-and-twenty. Had Percy Forbes ever spoken freely about her to any one in those days, he would have added, "And, my God, what will she be when she is old?"

Heart, and soul, and body, she was a flirt; not an innocent harmless flirt, like many a girl who settles down after a time into a sufficiently sober and discreet matronhood—but a flirt ingrain, a flirt who did not care at what price her success was purchased, what tears flowed, what wounds were inflicted, so as she was satisfied—she triumphant.

She had her grievance against society; but whatever of pain and mortification she had received, she paid back through the years with interest.

She had not been born in the purple, and the purple was slow about recognising her merits.

She had received slights: great ladies had

been insolent to her, as only, perhaps, great ladies know how.

They had wounded her pride—they had criticised her manners—they had refused to admit her into the holy of holies. "Fast" was not a word much in vogue in the days of which I am writing, but Miss Alwyn was considered the equivalent of fast, and looked coldly on accordingly.

Therein, however, society made a mistake—as great a mistake as it made about Mr. Alwyn's wealth.

Could Miss Alwyn have gone a pace, there is no doubt but she would gladly have astonished all the dowagers of her acquaintance; but there were so few things of the nature of speed within her reach, that perforce she was obliged to travel quietly enough along the road of life.

She could not drive; she dare no more have attempted to guide a pair of ponies even from Mallingford to the station, than she could have flown. If there was one thing she earnestly desired, it was nerve and skill sufficient to enable her to become a good whip and a good rider. She had persisted in attempting to manage a horse, spite of her own fears and the warnings of those who were learned in such matters. She had her ambition and her weakness, and both had received a severe shock, when she and Firefly and Lawrence Barbour lay in a heap together within the sight of Piccadilly.

She desired to do everything well, and there were many things which she could not do at all.

Discovering this, she bemoaned her fate at not having been rich from her youth upwards, at not having been put on a pony in her infant days; in not having been used to horses all her life; in not having moved in the best society from her childhood; in not having been taught by the greatest artists how to play like Thalberg, and sing like Grisi.

"God is very good," Percy Forbes was wont to tell her; "if you had been too perfect, you would not have given any other woman a chance. No doubt it was wisely ordered, or we might all have been too fond of you."

And then Etta would flash round on him, and answer—

"Have you not been too fond of me, Percy? Have you not——"

"Yes; I plead guilty," he was wont to reply: "but I will never be too fond of you again, Hetty. Make yourself quite easy on that score, for I never will."

"I wonder at you, Percy; I wonder how you dare——"

"And so do I, sweetest, wonder how I ever escaped with life; wonder how, loving you as I once did, I ever can have come to love you not at all. Spare your pains, Hetty; keep your trouble for some one else, for I vow to you, I vow and I declare—you might as well try now to touch the heart of the dead, as the heart of Percy Forbes."

"Your heart is not dead," she would answer, scornfully.

"And did I say it was? Did you desire to kill me altogether? Did you want not to leave me a chance of escape, not even a little city to flee unto ? Dearest Hetty, you are very beautiful, but you are also very wicked, and very cruel; as I said before, the Almighty has been good to mankind in not suffering you to have too much power over weak saints like myself."

They quarrelled, this pair; quarrelled eternally; and yet Henrietta was fond of Percy Forbes, and would fain have kept him at her feet for ever.

It was a sight to see the pair wrangling and disputing,—to behold how coolly Percy caught all her sneers and flung them back at her,—how she got crimson with passion, and, while she hurled taunts at him, dilated with a rage which she was impotent to express.

She was tall, and had a glorious figure; she had a skin as white and as pure as the flower of a lily; she had got masses of black hair, which hung in curls over neck and shoulders — in twining curls, that seemed to have life in them, that were, as Percy said, less like the flowing locks of a woman than the coils of a snake. She had small hands and feet, her head was well set on, and she bore herself with a haughty and defiant carriage.

She had regular features: a somewhat large mouth, with full, red lips, and eyes—what colour were her eyes?—that kept changing, changing like a cat's, as the varying light fell upon them.

Women she did not like, and, for that matter, she professed not to like men either; but women certainly were her abhorrence, and the lady who presided over the establishment in Hereford Street, and who was *chaperone*, companion, housekeeper, all in one, could have testified to the truth of Henrietta's statement out of the fullness of her own experience.

Further, she might have added that women did not like Miss Alwyn; which was the less to be wondered at, if the saying that love begets love be correct.

Very vague and very shadowy are these figures on my paper. It is merely the negatives which have been taken, but perhaps as the story proceeds the faces and the forms may grow more distinct, and stand out clearly as photographs before the eye of the reader.

It was after the fashion of photographs that father, and daughter, and house, came to be stamped in time on the memories of Lawrence Barbour and Percy Forbes.

Many a man and many a woman came and went and faded out of their recollection, but the features of Mr. Alwyn and his daughter never grew faint or cloudy on their mental canvas.

There were dwellings, once familiar, which became as strange habitations to them in the course of years, and streets that their feet once traversed frequently, grew in time to be forgotten localities; but Hereford Street, and the house therein, where Henrietta and her father abode, remained as ink upon paper, as carving on a rock, with both men to the end.

It is not likely that Hereford Street is a region of the West End well known to many who read these pages. It was never much of a thoroughfare, running as it did parallel with Oxford Street.

Running as it did! for alas! here, too, all is changed: where there were houses there is now a space of waste ground; the south side of the street is demolished, and where Mr. Alwyn's opposite neighbours lived and died, ate and drank, married and gave in marriage, feasted and fasted, there is at this moment a little tract of desert land enclosed with low wooden palings looking wretched and desolate in the twilight.

Part of the north side remains for the present intact, but changed almost past recognition.

The front-doors of the former time are the back-doors of the present; entrances have been made from Oxford Street, and the dining-rooms of the years gone by are filled with goods and desecrated by the voices of buyers and sellers.

Still, however, the house is standing where Mr. Alwyn lived and was great; and if a man be at all imaginative, he may, in the evening fire-light, people the now deserted rooms with their former inhabitants. He can fancy that the years have not gone by, bringing changes with them; he can listen for the stopping of carriages at doors that only now open to take in the milk; he can assign one apartment to this purpose and another to that; he can fill the balconies with flowers, and see the guests trooping down the stone staircase to dinner; he can assign a corner at the end of the drawing-room to the grand piano; he can place couches on each side the hearth; he can wait for the ladies coming up from an apartment hung with crimson flock-paper on the ground-floor, where a repast, not *à la Russe*, has just been served; he can pass through a much ornamented door-way, and peep into what was once a sleeping-chamber beyond; he can see the old-fashioned four-poster, hung with heavy draperies, and look at his own face in the mirror placed between the windows, in which beauty was wont to smile at the reflection of her own loveliness.

There are still the much ornamented ceilings, —still the richly-carved doorways,—still the mouldings, the cornices, the marks of where pictures have been hung, the old, old-fashioned chimney-pieces, where sienna is let into the

white slab, and carried round the edges of the
fireplace. There are the marble hearths, and the
high grates of former days; there is the imitation-
oak staining on the floor, marking just where the
carpet was laid; there is the skirting round the
room, finished off with much care, and a vast
amount of moulding; there are the panelled
doors; there is carving everywhere—on the
wainscot, on the window-shutters, on the en-
tablatures and jambs of the doorways. What more
could a dreamer desire than to sit in such a room,
in the firelight, and bid the men and the women
who formerly peopled it appear again unto
him?

They come out of the gloom! out of the darkness, they come and stand in groups about the
hearth, laughing, chatting, flirting as of old.
They come, and he looks in their faces, and sees
those in their youth who are now old, those old
who are now dead.

He recalls the hopes and the fears, the joys
and the sorrows of each; hopes never fulfilled,
and forgotten fears that will trouble them no

more; joys that have passed away, sorrows that they have taken to the grave with them.

Love, despair, anger, remorse, laughter, tears —all these have found a resting-place within the walls, that are now bare of life.

Let us away, friends, let us away from the house that now is, to the house that was; let us rise, and put the phantom host to rout with the presence of honest flesh and blood; let us leave the deserted rooms to the spectres of the past, and enter them no more, save when they are furnished and inhabited, with the men and the women who have each in this story a part to play out.

So! darkness is settling down upon the passages and the landing as we walk forth from the drawing-room, and pass down the stairs, and when we close the hall-door, which is now so seldom opened, behind us, and steal out into the saddening twilight, we leave the old house empty, and the once cheerful apartments without a living thing in them to take away the sense of desolation utter and complete!

CHAPTER XIII.

THROUGH the glorious summer weather Lawrence Barbour lay in hospital.

Into the wards of St. George's the sun streamed brightly; from the windows of the hospital the convalescents could see Hyde Park and the Queen's gardens full of leaf, and green with verdure. The Row was by no means deserted; the Drive was thronged day after day with carriages; along Piccadilly and down the Knightsbridge Road the stream of human life poured continually; the water-carts spread a pleasant coolness on the streets as they went by; there were trucks full of flowers that looked gay in the middle of the London thoroughfares; whichever way one turned there were cool muslins and light silks and white straw bonnets; the parks were alive with children; there was no frost, no mud, no fog; the pleasantest time of all the year to be in the Great Babylon had come; the best season for seeing London, its palaces, its churches, its squares, its bridges, its docks, its shipping, its river, its long, long lines of streets, its suburbs, its crowded resorts, had arrived; but still Lawrence lay, as I have said, in hospital, creeping his way back by slow degrees to comparative health.

That was a part cut out of his life; he learned no useful lesson; he acquired no sweet virtue; he failed both in patience and gratitude. It was a blank page on which, in the after days, he never could perceive that any beneficial line had been traced.

Thankless and uneasy, he often turned his tired eyes towards the light, murmuring, "Would it not have been better, O Lord, to have taken me at once than to leave me to drag on my life thus?" but he never, at any stage of his illness, so far bowed his heart as to say, " God's will be done."

Well, it was hard. There is nothing harder than to bear; and that was all the work Lawrence had set him to do at the time of which I am writing.

He was young, and the young always grudge the loss of even an hour of their existence. He was naturally active, and it is not easy for an active man to lie by with equanimity. He was willing to work, and the sole labour allotted to him was idleness. Morning after morning the sun rose and shone into the wards; day after day the summer brightness gladdened the London streets : patients went and came continuously; men left their legs behind them, and departed ; had their arms set, and were made sound again : recovered from the effects of frightful accidents, and walked away in company with their friends; but still he lay on, and thought his thoughts, and. bore his pain in silence.

Visitors not a few came and sat by him. Mr Alwyn did his duty of course ; and Lord Lallard was very kind and considerate to the son of his old neighbour, calling in often to cheer him up with news of the outer world, and asking him to go down and stay at Lallard Park for a time, whenever he was able to travel.

Mr. Barbour did not return to town after his first visit. Travelling was expensive, and his interviews with Lawrence had not, as a whole, been productive of pleasure or satisfaction to either; he resented Mr. Alwyn's attempts to force his hospitality on him as insolent condescension, and Mr. Perkins's well-meaning proffers of friendship as impertinent familiarity.

He had told his son he considered starvation preferable to such association, and entreated him to return home. To which Lawrence had answered, " Each one to his taste; for my part, I had rather beg in the London streets, than go mouching in idleness about the Clay Farm as I used to do."

After a very few such passages, Mr. Barbour wended his sorrowful way back to Mallingford, feeling that the business taint brought into the blood of his family by Miss Perkins would never be obliterated; and when on the following Sunday a sermon was delivered on "Original Sin," the disappointed gentleman associated in his own mind the fall of Adam and the marriage of his great-grandfather with the drysalter's daughter.

He turned his hopes next on Edmund, who certainly had developed no trading propensities, but this was unfortunately rather because he was idle, than because he was proud; rather because he detested work of any kind, than because he desired to push himself on, and rise to eminence in any other pursuit or profession.

Lawrence was the son who could have brought green leaves and goodly fruit on the bare and barren family tree—Lawrence, and he would not! He had chosen his own road in life, and was resolved to follow it to the end! What wonder that Mr. Barbour left London disgusted and disappointed, and tried to forget that evil for which indeed there seemed no remedy?

He had his paternal feelings however, never-theless, and wrote frequently to his first-born, pressing on him to come home for a time; at least, till his health should be re-established.

Mr. Sondes—the only person Mr. Barbour had seen in London whom he could endure, and in whose house, far east though it might be, he had been good enough to stay—answered these letters on behalf of the patient, and softened down, as he wrote, all those harshnesses of expression for which Lawrence was famous.

In due time, also, Edmund managed to scrape together enough money to come up and see London and the invalid. Which spectacle he enjoyed most, it would perhaps be invidious to inquire.

As for the Perkinses, there was neither be-ginning nor end of them, for Mrs. Perkins, greatly to Lawrence's distress, considered it incumbent upon her to visit him in his affliction, and made up little parties for the purpose of inducing him to, as she phrased it, forget his "troubles a bit."

In this laudable object Mrs. Perkins succeeded to admiration. No other person who ever entered St. George's ever caused Lawrence so thoroughly to lose all sense of his bodily ailments as the chemist's wife.

She called him a "poor dear," and kissed him with motherly demonstrativeness. She sat with his hand in hers till both got clammy and wet, when Lawrence could endure such marks of affection and attention no longer. She brought him the most wonderful cakes, the most astonishing delicacies, the stalest of fruits. She wore hideous bonnets, and either a white or a crimson shawl; she had always a child with her : in fact, the children looked upon Lawrence's illness as something rather agreeable and productive of excitement, and were much vexed and troubled in spirit when, by reason of his recovery, the pleasant pilgrimages to Hyde Park Corner ceased.

Sometimes Mrs. Jackson accompanied her friend, and then indeed Lawrence wondered why women so ugly were allowed to live, why women with such tongues were not gagged and got rid of.

Ada, too, assisted at these ceremonies with great vivacity and loquacity. At an early stage of the proceedings, viz., on the occasion of her first visit, she climbed up on the bed, thereby occasioning Lawrence such agony that he damned the engaging child so heartily and loudly, as to bring the nurse to his side, and cause the whole ward to be convulsed with smothered laughter.

He endeavoured subsequently to apologize to Mrs. Perkins for his warmth, but his excuses were unnecessary—Mrs. Perkins having already taken his part to the extent of threatening to inflict punishment on Miss Ada when she got her home, and of declaring to the offender that she would tell her "par of her goings on," who would never, never let her come to see her "poor, dear, sick cousin again."

"Now, if she only holds to that," thought Lawrence, while Ada put up her shoulders and dropped her under lip, and swelled out her cheeks,

and got very red in the face : all preparatory
signs of a thorough good sobbing fit.

"If you let her cry, you will both be turned
out," exclaimed Lawrence, wildly regardless of
whether there were any truth in his statement or
not; "they won't allow any noise here." Whereupon Ada was desired to behave herself, and
gulped back her grief accordingly.

Unhappily for Lawrence, however, Mrs. Perkins
did not prove as good as her word, for she brought
Ada, not merely again, but frequently; and Ada
invariably came into the ward bearing in her
hands a huge bunch of flowers, which she presented to her cousin.

These flowers were scentless, limp, and long-
gathered, as it is the nature of London flowers—
of the commoner sort—to be; further, the stalks
were wet and sticky, which last fact was to be
attributed to the persistency with which Ada had
eaten sweets all the way in the Blackwall omnibus
which conveyed her and her mother from Limehouse to Piccadilly.

Then there were occasional incursions of

the younger children, who surveyed Lawrence with astonished interest, and asked Mrs. Perkins,—

"What made his face so white, like chalk, and his eyes so big, and his bones so plain, and his voice so queer?"

"Is he soon going to die?" asked the youngest but one, the first time he was permitted to look on Lawrence after his accident.

The child had sat silent for many minutes, staring at his relative, and occupying that vantage post of observation, his mother's lap, must have arrived at the above result by a slow and careful course of reasoning, the cleverness of which Mrs. Perkins seemed unable to appreciate, for she declined to gratify his curiosity, and desired him to "Hush!" declaring, in the same breath, that children should "be seen and not heard."

Lawrence mentally amended this sentence. He thought children ought to be neither seen nor heard; and the "same rule would hold good with regard to many grown-up people too," he finished, having in his mind's eye more especially Mrs. Perkins, who had a pernicious habit of taking off her gloves, and pulling them out finger, by finger, of unfastening her bonnet-strings and setting that article of attire very far back on her head, of throwing off her shawl, and remarking with vehemence on the heat, breathing deep sighs, at intervals, expressive of being oppressed and weary; weary with fanning herself with her pocket-handkerchief, perhaps, for that was a duty in which she never relaxed voluntarily.

Ah! belles and ladies of fashion, could you but see how your little affectations—how your airs and graces, your habits, your attitudes, your foibles, are imitated and caricatured by the vulgar herd; how in omnibuses, in second-class railway carriages, in steamboats, in the back seats in church, ay, in your servants' halls, women are all engaged in doing ill that which it is your patent of nobility to do well, viz., making themselves artificial, and as far as possible from what God intended they should be ;—would it, I wonder, induce you to fall back on the graces of simplicity, on the beauties of perfect naturalness ?

Percy Forbes, who was in the habit of coming often to St. George's and watching with somewhat cynical eyes the ways and manners of *le beau sexe* as there exhibited, took a delight in noticing how the lower class aped the weaknesses of the higher, and in declaring that women, rich or poor, high or low, were all alike.

He was hard upon wives and daughters, this young man with the chestnut hair and the brownish-grey eyes, which seemed the less excusable, since wives and daughters kept each and all a pleasant look and word for him.

He had his ideal possibly of what a woman ought to be; but if so, certainly none amongst his acquaintances came up to his requirements. Decidedly not Mrs. Perkins, at any rate, whom he often had the felicity of meeting, and to whom he was christian and courteous even to the extent of accompanying her out of the hospital, and walking forth with her into

Grosvenor Place and hailing an omnibus for her, and handing her and whatever child she had brought to see Lawrence into the same, and lifting his hat to her when the conductor banged his foot on the step, or slapped the panel with his strap, signalling thereby to the driver that he could go on: just, Mrs. Perkins was wont to remark to her husband, "as if I was a countess."

Altogether Mrs. Perkins was charmed with both the young men, for Lawrence seldom failed in outward civility. There were some things, however, which he could not have done even out of politeness. For instance, he could not have voluntarily escorted Mrs. Perkins up Piccadilly. In this respect Percy had the advantage over him, and perhaps Lawrence did not like his new friend any the better for it. Nevertheless, the two young men had become friends after a fashion, and spent a considerable amount of time talking together on various subjects.

Mr. Sondes also often travelled westward to

see his *protégé*, and never entered St. George's without a lovely bouquet, hidden away in moss, which Olivine sent to Lawrence with her love.

Those were the sweetest flowers that reached the sick man in his extremity—pure, and fresh, and sweet, and cool, and simple; not too rare to touch, not overpowering in their rich fragrance; not arranged to order by the hands of a gardener who tied them up with bass, as was the case with the bouquets from Mallingford, but just a sprig or two, a few buds nestling among moss, grateful to the sense, refreshing to the eye, green and bright as though that moment gathered, grouped together simply yet daintily, as it was in the child's nature to group everything which her hands touched.

She lived in the country all through the hot summer weather, in an old-fashioned house down by the river edge, some five-and-twenty miles from town; and the flowers and the moss told tales to the invalid lying in hospital, of the fields and the trees which he was debarred from seeing.

Not that Lawrence loved the country much, or sighed greatly after its delights; only, when he was restless and feverish the flowers seemed to talk to him of rest and shade, just as the sound of running water is grateful at times to a man who, it may be, loves best to drink wine.

One cannot tell how or why these things make any impression on apparently unimpressionable people; we only know the effect is produced, and wonder to remark it. And the effect produced on Lawrence Barbour was to make him long almost passionately to get out of hospital, to flee away, not to Lallard Park, nor to Mallingford End, nor to Clay Farm, nor to Ramsgate, as Mr. Perkins suggested, but to Grays, where Mr. Sondes had a house that commanded a view of the river, and from which you could see the ships going up and down with their sails all set and shining in the morning sunshine.

Now Lawrence had never seen the river, except from London or some of the other bridges, and once from Grays, on that occasion mentioned by Mrs. Jackson to Mrs. Perkins. He had never sat beside a window idly looking over a great expanse of water: never beheld the sun rising upon and setting over it; never watched it in storm and calm, in daylight and in the deepening twilight. He was not an imaginative man; but he had every element in him for becoming a solitary one; and therefore it happened, perhaps, that in his sickness the idea took firm hold of his mind if he could but get away to Grays he should soon be restored to health,—to comparative health, as has before been said. He wanted to run off from London, to be clear of Mr. Alwyn, and Mrs. Perkins, and doctors, and nurses, and diet, and the sight of illness and suffering; he was sick of the hot days and of the hotter nights; he longed for the river breeze, for the solitary bedchamber, for the cool grass, for the fresh wind to come and fan his temples. And so the days went by—the days and the weeks; and late on in the summer he walked feebly out of St. George's—cured.

CHAPTER XIV.

A LITTLE SURPRISE.

Cured! Very bitterly Lawrence Barbour repeated that word to himself as he drove along Piccadilly and across Leicester Square, and so by the Strand and through the City back to Limehouse.

He felt giddy with the unwonted motion of the cab ; the noise of the streets irritated his nerves. By the time he had reached Tichbourne Street he was faint and sick and weary, but still, cured. The doctors had done all they could for their patient—given him what measure of health it was in their power to bestow, and discharged him sound and strong as it was likely he would ever be.

The human machine had been repaired to the

uttermost; the instrument had been put in such
tune as was possible after the jar it had sustained; but the machine could never work again
so smoothly as had once been the case, the instrument might never more give forth so strong a
tone as formerly, let the man's life be long or let
it be short.

"And this is being cured," he said, feebly, as
the cab jolted along over the stones down King
William Street and so into the Strand. "This
is being cured. Last time I passed this way I
was well and strong as anybody need to be; I
did not know what it was to have ache or pain,
and now—the clothes in which I left Limehouse
that day are literally hanging upon me, and I
could not walk even from your house to Stepney
Causeway if I were offered all the gold in the
Bank of England for doing so."

"You will mend of that," answered Mr.
Perkins, cheerily. Mr. Perkins had come to
fetch his relative out of the hospital, and now
sat beside him in the cab. "You will mend of
that. You must eat well, and drink well, and get

away either to Ramsgate or Grays; and then after that we will talk about your being cured, but not till then. You have had a nasty bout of it, and we must try to repair the damage done to your constitution."

"If Mrs. Perkins break a tea-cup she can send Jane out to buy another; but can she ever make the old cup sound again?" demanded Lawrence, peevishly.

"No," answered Mr. Perkins; "nobody ever thought she could; only, you see, the difference in this case is that you are not a tea-cup. It is dead and you are living; it is inanimate matter, with no physical power of repairing a waste; you are animate, and therefore have within your-self the capacity for acquiring fresh strength, for knitting broken bones, for making in course of time, in fact, a sound body out of an injured one. What is the use of looking at the worst side of things? If you were eighty the question might indeed be a different one; but you are young, healthy, naturally of a strong constitution, with good blood in your veins, and good sense in your head. Make use of that sense now, and ask yourself whether it is reasonable to suppose a man who has been in hospital for so long would feel strong enough to ride a steeple-chase the first day he gets out into the open air. The thing is absurd. Wait, as I have said, for a month, and then tell me how you feel about being broken up for life."

"But the doctors warned me," began Lawrence.

"Never mind their warnings," interrupted Mr. Perkins, "or at least only take them for what they are worth. Doctors are not infallible; doctors are not God Almighty, and no one but He can say for certain what time and rest and patience may not do for you yet. It is just possible," went on the chemist, with a delightful inconsistency, "that your chest may never be quite strong again; but what of that? How many people are going about the world now with delicate chests. How many have only a piece of a lung left to breathe through, and yet keep themselves alive winter after winter——"

"Ay, keep themselves alive," commented Lawrence. "I had rather be dead at once, than feel my breath pulling me back every step I took."

"But you have got both your lungs, and although they may not be very strong now, still——"

"Still the cracked cup lasts a long time if it be not much used," finished Lawrence. "That is the worst of it, Mr. Perkins; with my bread to win, with my way to make, I shall have to keep the fact of my broken health always in mind. Well, so be it; I have made my last complaint, I have uttered my last moan. I accept the inevitable, and will try to make the best of a bad bargain."

"That is right," remarked Mr. Perkins, "you will not find the bargain so bad an one after all. Are you getting very tired? It is an awful long drive for you to take for a beginning."

What Mr. Perkins said was perfectly true, and by the time Lawrence reached Distaff Yard, he felt glad enough to crawl up stairs and go straight away to bed.

"This is nice," he observed, as he laid his head on the pillow in his own little room again, —"this is nice," and that was the first approach to a really grateful speech which Mr. Perkins had heard him utter. "Do you want me to eat?" he added, "and I so comfortable." But he raised himself up for all that, and swallowed what Mr. Perkins gave him; and afterwards his relative closed the door and ordered the children downstairs, and left Lawrence to go to sleep.

Oh! the blessedness of that sleep—the happiness of lying with his eyes shut, all alone—the pleasure of waking, and not finding one on his right hand, and another on his left, suffering, and making lamentation.

It was late in the evening when he awoke, and then he only did so sufficiently to assure himself there was really no other occupant of the room, after which he dropped off to sleep again.

"Thank God," was his latest conscious thought, "that when we take our rest for the last time, we shall each have a separate coffin." It was a strange idea to come into a young man's head;

but then Lawrence Barbour was a strange young
man, who had been much accustomed to solitude
all his life, to whom nothing seemed so perfectly
unendurable as having people always about him,
and who spoke merely the simple truth the next
morning when he told Mrs. Perkins he had never
enjoyed anything so much before, as the past
night's sleep in Distaff Yard.

"And I am sure it has done you a world of
good," answered Mrs. Perkins; "and now, don't
you think, my dear, you could persuade Josiah to
let you and me and the children go down to
Ramsgate or Southend all together comfortably?
It would be ever so much better for you to be
with us than moping in that dull house at Grays,
alone with Mr. Sondes and Olivine. There
would be some life about my children, but nobody
ever saw a bit of life about her—not that I mean
to say Olivine is not a nice little girl enough, considering the unchristian way in which she has
been brought up—but still cheerfulness is one
thing and melancholy is another. My poor
father used always to be singing 'Away with

melancholy,'" concluded Mrs. Perkins, commencing forthwith to hum that remarkably difficult air all out of tune.

Lawrence made no answer. He lay still, considering that, if he went to the seaside with Mrs. Perkins and Ada, the journey might be considered an unnecessary expense. "I could go to Bedlam when I came back," he decided "but certainly to no other place."

He pictured to himself Ada scampering about the sands, and shuddered, as in a prophetic vision he saw her thick legs, her light hair, her upturned nose, her blue eyes, her forward manners, and her eternal giggle astonishing the Ramsgate visitors. Already he felt the weight of Mrs. Perkins' hand as she took hold of his arm, down whatever public promenade that place might boast. It was all very well to do the agreeable to Mrs. Perkins at Limehouse, but even to propose to his own mind the idea of doing the agreeable to Mrs. Perkins anywhere out of the locality in which her husband carried on his business was a thing not to be thought of.

Having decided this point by the time Mrs. Perkins had dusted his looking-glass, and shaken his toilet-cover, and put the room what she called "to-rights," Lawrence informed her he could not possibly get off going to Mr. Sondes', that he had promised to spend some time at Grays, whenever he was strong enough to travel anywhere.

"Oh! dear," exclaimed Mrs. Perkins, standing in the centre of the room, the very personification of household uncomeliness, and holding her duster tightly in her hand, and looking most grievously annoyed while she spoke, "Oh! dear; then there's no chance of me and the poor children getting away for a breath of fresh air before the summer is over. Mr. Perkins would have let us go, if you had gone, but now—but there, what is the use of talking about it? That Mr. Sondes is the antidote, or bane, or whatever you call it, of my life. There is nothing I want he does not put his foot in somehow. I don't blame you, of course; but it is provoking, now, confess yourself, isn't it? Here I am month after month,

slave, slave, slave—worse than any negro. I am
.sure I earn every bite and sup crosses my lips.
What other woman with a family like mine, and
Josiah in business on his own account, would do
with only one servant, and her a fool! I cook,
and iron, and have his food always wholesome
and hot, and the children have never a hole in
their stockings, and the house is as clean as a
new pin, and I am up every morning as soon as
the men get to work; but I might just as well be
a slut and a lie-a-bed, and waster, and extravagant, for all the thanks I have. It is that Mr.
Sondes' doing—all—every bit. Likely as not he
knew I wanted to go to Ramsgate or Southend,
and made up his mind I shouldn't. He knows
everything,—perhaps what I am saying to you at
this present minute. Well, let him know then;
listeners never hears no good of themselves,"
said Mrs. Perkins, by way of ending to her
speech, which had got not merely illogical, but
ungrammatical towards its conclusion, by reason
of the vehemence of her feelings. "They never
does," and Mrs. Perkins aimed a blow at an

imaginary cobweb depending from the ceiling, while Lawrence remarked,—

"That he was positive if Mr. Perkins knew she wanted to go out of town, he would make no objection to her doing so," to which straight-forward speech Mrs. Perkins made answer, "Much you know about it,—much you know about what husbands object to ; not but what, in his way, Josiah is good enough in the main, only I would rather never set foot beyond the doors, than worry and torment like some wives. I don't want to go out often. I had just as lief stay here, but the children, poor dears, will be disappointed ; ay, that they will."

Now what was Lawrence to do ? He felt guiltily conscious in the matter, so conscious, in fact, that he said, after a pause and a struggle,—

"Mrs. Perkins, if you wish so much to go to Ramsgate, and can only get there if I accompany you, I will explain the state of the case to Mr. Sondes, and ——"

"No, thank you, Mr. Barbour," she interrupted ; "I don't want to be under no obligations

to Mr. Sondes for nothing; and it is of no consequence to me—further than wishing you well,
and thinking your visit to a person who wants to
marry you to his niece a mistake—where you go
to stay, whether in that dismal old house at
Grays, or in nice genteel lodgings at Ramsgate,
or, well, say—Southend."

"Marry me to his niece," Lawrence repeated.
He never heard a word after that clause of the
sentence. Mrs. Perkins's telling contrasts had
been lost upon him.

"Marry me to his niece! what niece?"

"What niece?—why Olivine; he has no other
that ever I heard of."

"But she is only a child."

"I know that she is only a child now, but she
will be a woman some day, if she lives long
enough."

"And I, if I ever do marry, will not until I am
forty."

"Trust you for that," observed Mrs. Perkins.

"You may trust me, for I have a notion that
when people marry so young they get tired of it,

somehow; besides, Mr. Sondes would not want a pauper as I am for a nephew-in-law. I do wish Mrs. Perkins, you would put that notion out of your mind. I cannot imagine how it ever got there."

"It is not into my mind alone it has got, let me tell you," answered Mrs. Perkins. "There's Mrs. Jackson (a sensible woman she is, too) as is quite of my opinion. She said no later than last night, setting comfortably over her tea, and me on the other side of the table listening to her —'Mark my words, Mrs. Perkins,' she says, 'that'll be a match some day.'

"'What'll be a match?' I asked, knowing all the time who she meant.

"'Why, between your young gentleman,' she says, 'and little Sondes.'"

"I wish to heaven Mrs. Jackson would mind her own business, and leave mine alone," said Lawrence, angrily.

"But she is just like her neighbours, and people won't leave your business alone," answered Mrs. Perkins.

"Well, then, they shall hold their tongues to me about it," he retorted. "How would you, Mrs. Perkins, like any one to say that you wanted to marry me to Ada?"

In a moment Lawrence perceived the error he had committed; in an instant he saw that such a report would not have been far from the truth; and he hurried on without waiting for any reply,

"The one thing is quite as absurd as the other; I have got my way to make in the world, to grow rich and independent; by the time my hair is grey I may think of taking to myself a wife, but I do not mean to clog my steps at present. And another thing I am confident of, is, that Mr. Sondes will either expect his niece to marry high or not at all."

But, although he said this, Mr. Lawrence Barbour's vanity was flattered at the idea of being considered already eligible. Two future brides growing up for him; a mother and an uncle deciding that it would be a "good match" for their girls. Vanity is a feeling easily awakened, difficult to kill; and Mrs. Perkins had something to answer for in making this youth look favourably on his own perfections.

He had heard of men educating wives for themselves; why should Mr. Sondes not desire to educate a husband for his niece? After all, might there not be a grain of truth at the bottom of Mrs. Perkins's bushel of chaff. It was pleasant to him to think so, at all events, and though he professed to be very indignant about the matter, still there can be no doubt but that, on the whole he felt a good deal flattered, and less than ever inclined to take up his abode in genteel lodgings at Ramsgate in company with Mrs. Perkins and her progeny.

Still, he was sorry for the woman's disappointment, and told her so; to which she replied that "sorrow was poor sauce," a statement Lawrence felt himself in no position to contradict, although he took an early opportunity of opening his mind to Mr. Sondes on the subject of the Ramsgate trip.

"She is a vulgar wretch," replied that gentleman; "but still, I suppose she requires a little change and variety as much as any lady in the land. I will speak to Perkins about it ;" and he did, with such good effect, that, before a week had passed, Miss Ada was digging graves for herself on the shore at Ramsgate, and jumping in and out of them with much of what she doubtless considered lightness and agility, while Mrs. Perkins alternately quarrelled with her landlady and ate shrimps in quantity. As for the younger children, the visit proved one of torment to them, for they were bathed, were dipped, shrieking and kicking in the sea, and borne, red in the face, and bordering on convulsions, back to the machine, where their mamma stood triumphantly waiting to receive them in an elegant undress of wet blue serge.

Whilst his family were thus enjoying themselves, Mr. Perkins "stuck to business," and Lawrence went down to spend the remainder of the summer in that house at Grays which Mr. Sondes had taken for the sake of Olivine.

CHAPTER XV.

AT GRAYS.

For the benefit of those readers who have patiently followed the course of this unromantic story up to the present point, it may be well to explain where Grays is, seeing that the place wherein Mr. Sondes abode, during all the bright summer months mentioned in previous chapters, happens to this day, to be one little frequented by Londoners.

It is not difficult of access. It is within an hour of the city; the air is pure and bracing, the country around is open and pleasant; it lies down by the river, and from the low rising ground beside the town you can see the Thames beneath, flowing on golden and shining in the sun. Nearly opposite, though a little more to the east, lies

Gravesend ; nearly opposite,—this time, however, a little to the west,—is Greenhithe, and on the same side of the river as " Grays Thurrock " itself, and south-by-east of the town, we find Tilbury, where the four pro-consular ways made by the Romans crossed each other.

Grays, the attentive reader will conclude from all this, is on the north bank of the Thames, and boasts a station on the Tilbury line. Even to the present day Grays Thurrocks is a very small place, consisting, in fact, but of one street, the houses in which are built principally of wood. For its size, however, it contains more hotels, or, to speak with greater correctness, hostelries, than any other town in England. Further, there are a larger number of outfitters' shops than a chance visitor might suppose could hope to find customers, every ordinary necessary and luxury of life seeming to be subservient to the clothes and et-ceteras needful for a sea-voyage—to boxes, blankets, pea-jackets, ropes, flannel-vests, and such like.

There is a small church surrounded by a large

burying-ground, the former of which had some additions made to it within the last twenty years, and is having some further additions made to it now. Even the oldest portion of the building is far from old, and can bear no comparison in point of interest and architectural beauty with the lonely church of West Thurrock, that lies away by itself in the fields, within sight of the river, and has not a dwelling-place near it, save the habitations of the dead.

Many vessels put into Grays, which fact accounts for the taverns and the outfitters; also, perhaps, for the wonderful little pies exhibited on deal boards in some of the windows, and a tarry smell about the lower portion of the town that greets the nose of the new-comer. Human ships also occasionally put into Grays—ships which may never cross the seas of life more—for the churchyard is, as I have said, large, and many a stranger lies buried there, who scarcely thought, when he was starting in existence, of the quiet port wherein he should eventually find shelter and rest.

Here, too, the gravestones bear frequently the merest record of a great tragedy.

"Unfortunately drowned" is the inscription on one, and indeed what need of more? What man who has ever seen the great depths, and listened to the howling of the winter wind, but can supply the rest? Mother earth has taken to her arms dead, those who left her living, and laps them up tenderly and lovingly with the soft green turf, while they sleep the sleep that may know no waking till Eternity.

It must be a wild bleak place in the winter time, this Gray Thurrock, when the storms beat the staggering vessels in here for shelter, and the wild wind speeds flying over the green hillocks and the flat lands down by the shore.

It must be fearfully exposed, and cold, and dreary, and desolate then; but in the summer season it is a sweet spot; pleasant and open, as before stated, and with a cool refreshing breeze generally blowing off the water, or across the lonely country that lies around. It is a nice place even now, in the summer time, for children who love the green fields;—but it was a nicer place still in the days when Lawrence Barbour knew it, for the bricks were not then moulded which have since built the few rows of cockney houses that spoil the neighbourhood; the chalk pits were still lying unquarried, and labourers' cottages, such as are now erected in Argent Street and on the hill-side, beyond the house where Mr. Sondes dwelt—were not needed.

There was no spick-and-span new brewery: there were no wharves; the staring two-storey houses, with their front gardens fenced round with walls built of crags, now cover ground where, in the days of which I am writing, the grass grew and the corn waved.

Well, people must live, and people must be housed; and there are plenty of green fields still left, thank God—enough, at any rate, to gladden your eyes and mine, reader, even at Grays, where we can look east and west and south, and behold mile after mile of lonely country with scarcely a house, while the river runs on beside the fields that lie close down to its brink; and away on the other side are the Kentish hills, and there is a great hush in the air, a silence that a Londoner, accustomed to the noise and rattle of the busy streets, feels, and marvels at.

To this place came Lawrence Barbour to recruit his health. As a horse who has met with some grievous accident in the first fifty yards is sent back to paddock, there to be nursed and seen to, so Lawrence, stricken down almost before his race for wealth had begun, travelled to Grays, hoping that the fresh air and the thorough rest and the unutterable repose of that quiet retreat would, as Mr. Perkins phrased it, make a man of him again.

Over the roofs of the houses, on a level with which the train sped along, he looked with a vague wondering interest, marvelling what history each dwelling contained; past the cemetery —then not so full of graves as it is now—he was swept within sight of many a manufactory, of endless chemical works, of countless factories, the engine laboured away ; but at last came the open country—the blessed country, and Lawrence, lying back in his carriage, could have cried for very joy at being free again—for very sorrow, because he might never look on the face of nature more, feeling just the same as formerly —as strong, as sound, as healthy as of yore.

Fields, and still more fields; miles without a house; a country as flat as an Irish bog but not so desolate, because the marshes are green, and lie also well exposed to the sun, which shines cheerily across them. Here and there a home-stead, with its few trees, with its great stacks of hay, with its cattle grazing or lying still in the splendour of the summer afternoon; past Bark-ing, leaving Dagenham, where, far to the right, it is said stood the house wherein the egg of the Gunpowder Plot was laid by the conspirators; on through Rainham, and so to Purfleet, which would be one of the loveliest spots round London for a pic-nic, were it not for the proximity of the Government magazines; then more fields—miles, and miles, and miles of them—and the line and the river approach closer to each other, and Lawrence, straining his eyes, could see over the flat lands, the Thames, like a silver thread, winding away among the grass, while the hills on the south side came nearer and nearer every moment.

At this point the country on the right-hand side of the down-line is so flat that all idea of distance and size is lost. It is only by the gleaming of the river, wide though it be, that the traveller can tell there is water between him and the rising grounds in Kent; thousands of acres of marsh-land, without tree or house, or hedge or ditch; great tracts of country over which the Thames has played, from time to time, strange tricks; then the church of West Thurrocks, standing in a position so lonely, that Lawrence began to marvel whether any congregation were ever collected within its walls, or if the dead rose from their graves, and trooped, a weird and ghastly procession, in their shrouds through the door and into the building at sound of the Sab-beth bells; after that, coming nearer and nearer to the river, Grays, with its small station, with its few passengers, either alighting or proceeding—

Grays, where Mr. Sondes met him, and conveyed him in a phaeton to the house he had taken for the season.

It was a charming abode, standing on the top of a hill, from whence you could see down over the town of Grays, and all the open country stretching away to the south-east; while the Thames lay below—so still, so tranquil, under the summer's sun, that it looked less like a river than like a lake.

The house is still there, but changed. Where were hedgerows are houses; where was a garden is a brickfield; but there is a private road still up to the close gates, that seem the fashion in that part of the country; and beyond the road a pleasant footpath leads across the fields, just as it used to do.

By the hall-door stood Olivine ready to welcome the visitor. There was something pleasant and homelike in the figure of the child; something that struck back to Lawrence's heart bitterly in the day of his blackest repentance.

Unconsciously the mind receives all kinds of

impressions without the slightest act of volition on the part of the spectator; every variety of picture is stamped on our brains, and we never know till the light falls hither and thither what scenes we have gathered up and stored in our memories, for good or for evil, for joy or for sorrow.

It was thus with Lawrence Barbour: there stood the child, with her dog at her side, with her kitten, now grown into a great cat, in her arms, looking up in his face with those sweet lovely eyes, into which there came tears as she gazed: there was Olivine, to whom he had sung his songs in the old house at Stepney, waiting to greet him with the sunlight shining on her, with the flowers around her. Very gently she put the cat down and came forward shyly, and quietly as ever; but she clung to his hand and stroked it softly, and when he stooped to kiss her, she put her arm round his neck and began to cry.

The scene was stamped at the instant on his memory, and yet, as the days went by, the picture was thrust aside into the lumber-room of memory, and forgotten.

Time passed on and the years went by; but when the years had come and gone—come and gone, behold! he saw before him, clear and fresh as though that moment painted, the house and the child, the cat and the terrier. Once more he felt the soft hand stroking his —once again he kissed the pure young lips, and knew that she was crying because he looked so changed; and then—and then—he wished— oh! God, *how* he wished he could go back and live the years over for the second time, and, seeing light, leave the darkness behind him for ever.

There was no noise about Olivine's welcome; the child seemed to live in a sort of perpetual hush. Her tears were not as the tears of other girls of her age, and her joy was less like their joy even than her grief.

When Lawrence returned to Distaff Yard, Miss Ada greeted his arrival with dancing, clapping, pirouetting, and jumping, to an unlimited extent.

If he had been some kind of rare fruit which she was trying to bring down, her leaps could not have been higher or more persistent.

"Look at him! look at him!" she cried, till, it affords me pleasure to record, her father boxed her ears, and told her not to make such an "infernal fool of herself."

She climbed on a table and embraced him; she told her younger brother, "their cousin had not died yet;" she displayed more of her legs than even Lawrence had ever seen before; and she looked uglier than of old.

"I came to see you in the hospital," she said, a day or two after his return, climbing on the back of his chair, and imparting this piece of information to his very ear.

Whereupon Lawrence suddenly rose, and the interesting child was suddenly capsized, giving vent, as she went down, to such a shriek as brought Mrs. Perkins from the kitchen to inquire what was the matter.

"He went and done it on purpose," sobbed Miss Ada, snivelling the while as only a child with a snub nose can. " He got up and let the chair down upon me, and he is a brute, and I hate him."

Whereupon Lawrence felt it necessary to offer some explanation. " How was I to know she was standing on the rail of the chair?" he asked. "If she is hurt, I am sorry; but I could not help it. Never mind, Ada, the first time I go out I will buy you some sweetmeats." Pacified by which promise, Ada professed her sorrow for calling him a brute, and stated that she only said so because she had hurt her head.

Now with Olivine there was nothing of all this; she had no affectation, she had no schemes, she did not want to attract notice. With her little heart brimming full of affection she could have sat apart for hours, asking neither for word, nor look, nor sign; she could gather flowers, and lay them softly beside Lawrence, without ever drawing his attention either to them or herself; she could carry out the sofa-pillows for him to rest his head on when he lay stretched on the grass, and never say, " I thought you would like them;" she could bring him the books he wanted and never ask for a story out of them; she could carry his jelly and grapes and take no surreptitious mouthful, as was the manner of Miss Ada.

Once she prayed him to sing—that was the only thing she ever begged him to do for her; and the cry of bitterness which broke from her lips when he said, "Ah! Olivine, I am afraid my singing-days are over," was a thing to be remembered. "I do not think I shall ever be able to sing again," he went on, laying his hand on her head as she sat on the grass beside him; "you must learn to sing for me, will you, pet?"

"I will try," she answered sadly; "but then I am not clever, like you; uncle says you are clever, and I am not."

"You are clever," he said; "clever as a woman ever wants to be, and you must learn to sing for me, and I will lie and listen, so;" and he stretched himself out full length on the turf, while Olivine laughed and covered him with daisies, and told him he was very naughty and told fibs to frighten her.

"It is no fib, child," he replied. " I lost my voice for love of Miss Alwyn one day, in Hyde Park."

"Now I know you are telling stories," she said ; " because you don't love Miss Alwyn, not an atom."

" What makes you think that, little one ? " he asked.

"I don't think it—I know it. I heard you talking to uncle about her, and you said you hated her; and I thought then how wicked you were to hate anybody."

"What a saint it is!" remarked Lawrence. "Did you never hate anybody, Olivine ? Now, honour bright, did you not ? "

Olivine paused ; she cast round and about her short life, routed out the inhabitants of this dark corner and of that, before she answered, " No, I never did, though I once very nearly hated Ada Perkins."

" What dreadful sin had she committed ? " asked Lawrence, lazily.

" Well, you see," replied Olivine, confidentially, and looking round to discover if any one were listening; "she came to spend one after-noon with me——"

."I hear, Olivine, but I do not see," inter-rupted Lawrence, who loved to torment the child.

"She came, at any rate," went on Olivine, with a little pout, "and we were playing with the cat that begs, you know, beside the open window, and Ada took her up; but pussy would not stay with her, and always walked over from Ada to me. As fast as she came to me I gave her back to Ada, and as fast as I gave her to Ada pussy came to me, till at last Ada got cross, and said, 'You nasty ungrateful beast, you shall not stay with either of us,' and pitched her out from ever so high into the garden."

"And what did you do, then?" inquired Mr. Lawrence Barbour.

"Oh, I felt I don't know how! Nurse Mary says I tried to jump out of the window after pussy, but I don't remember that. I cannot remember anything except Ada crying and saying

she did not mean to hurt it; and then Nurse
Mary brought me pussy, safe and sound, and
after that she put me to bed, and when I awoke
pussy was asleep beside me. But I am afraid I
struck Ada," continued the child. "I am not
certain, and nobody would ever tell me; but I
think I struck her, and I never struck anybody
before; and if I did strike her, I could not
help it."

"Come and give me a kiss, Olivine," said
Lawrence, who enacted the grand seigneur in
those days, and had every person at his beck and
call. "I am sure you are a good child, and—
shall I tell you a secret?—I hate Ada Perkins
myself!"

"But you must not—it is wicked, it is bad; you
cannot go to Heaven if you hate."

"I shall have to take my chance of that,"
answered Lawrence, calmly; "this world is
enough for me."

He should not have uttered such a sentence in
the child's hearing, and next instant he knew he
had been wrong; for Olivine put her little hand

upon his mouth and " hushed " him, as though they had been standing in a church.

" Do not say that," she pleaded, " it is naughty, and you must not be naughty; please be good, please—please," and Olivine flung herself beside him, and threw such a tone of earnest entreaty into her voice, that Lawrence, struck with a sudden wonderment, answered,—

" It would be easy for any one to be good who was always near you, Olivine. I think you must be a child-angel, you are so perfect."

And he drew down the sweet face and kissed it once,—twice,—thrice, little deeming, as he did so, he was kissing in very truth the good angel of his life.

It was very happy, it was very innocent, it was very pleasant, but all at once Olivine started up, crying,—

" Oh ! Mr. Barbour, there are some strangers coming in ! I must go to Nurse Mary, and see who they are."

Nurse Mary, however, saved Olivine the

trouble, for she came forward into the garden at the moment, announcing,—

" Mr. and Miss Alwyn are in the drawing-room, to see Mr. Barbour."

CHAPTER XVI.

WITH anything rather than a good grace
Lawrence rose to his feet and prepared to obey
Nurse Mary's summons. Inwardly, he anathematised Mr. Alwyn, and Miss Alwyn, and all
visitors. In his heart of hearts he wished father
and daughter far enough; but still he rose and
walked into the house, and entered the drawing-
room, where Mr. Alwyn greeted him with a sort
of nervous cordiality.

"Taken you by storm, eh? Went first to
Distaff Yard, but found the bird flown; next
best thing that presented itself was to take the
train at Stepney and come on here. Mr. Lawrence Barbour—my daughter. Etta, you ought
to know this gentleman without my introduction."

At which plain hint Etta advanced and shook hands, putting on her most seductive smile, and saying in her softest voice,—

" I really do not know how to thank you, Mr. Barbour. I cannot tell you how grieved I am to think my safety should have been purchased at so terrible a price. *Are* you better? I *trust* you are." And Lawrence felt the hand she still suffered to lie in his, tremble, as Miss Alwyn asked this question.

Then, for the first time in his life, he experienced a strange and unwonted sensation.

He had looked at this girl often, previously, at a distance—he had mocked her riding—he had sneered at her hair—he had stared at her in church—he had mimicked and derided the siren whom he could not now find words to answer— before whom he now stood for a moment confounded and abashed.

" You look so pale," she went on ; " and I am *so* sorry. If I had been the one injured instead of you, how much better it would have been ; for you, papa tells me, are going to be a great worker, while I am but a cumberer of the ground."

"Nay, nay, Etta," interrupted Mr. Alwyn, who felt that perhaps this was going a little too far; while Lawrence answered, a little bitterly,—

"The humble creatures of this earth, Miss Alwyn, are for use, and the beautiful are for ornament. Men crush the useful, and admire the beautiful; and I am happy to have fulfilled the universal law and saved you from injury."

"What a cynic!" she remarked.

"No, I only speak the truth," he replied, and he raised his eyes and fixed them boldly on her. "I am happy to have been of use to you, though I did not feel there was any happiness in the matter five minutes since."

"Am I to accept that speech as a compliment?" she asked, trifling with the fastening of her glove, as she spoke.

"Not as a compliment," Lawrence answered, at which reply Mr. Alwyn laughed, and said,—

"Upon my honour, young gentleman, it is

a pity you were not born a courtier; for your speeches are fitter for a palace than for the homes of ordinary mortals. If Etta were not accustomed to flattery, I should beg you to remember she is but a merchant's daughter, and not a maiden of romance. As it is, however, I suppose she knows pretty well the value of such commodities, and prizes them accordingly."

Once more the blood rushed hot and swift through Lawrence's veins, and he would have stood up to do battle for the genuineness of his sentiments, but that Miss Alwyn interrupted him.

"On the contrary, papa," she remarked, "I prize Mr. Barbour's words exceedingly, feeling confident he really means what he says, which is more than I should venture to affirm concerning most of my acquaintances." And with that Miss Alwyn smiled once again sweetly on Lawrence, who felt inclined at the moment to turn and flee away.

"As a rule," a clever woman once informed

me, " we dislike people whom we do not know;" as a rule, likewise, I think, we instinctively recoil from those who are destined to work us evil. It is Nature's warning: it is her hand laid on us in appeal, it is her voice bidding us beware; and if we disregard the warning, the appeal, and the caution, what then? Why, then we are but as the moths who, put out at one window return through another, and are burnt in the flame before a hand can be stretched forth to save them!

Up to that time Lawrence had hearkened to the voice of his better angel, and remained resolutely deaf to all the seductive charms of Mr. Alwyn's discourse. Not that gentleman's polite and delicate attentions, not the hot-house flowers, not the rare fruits, not the pressing invitations to stay at Mallingford, not the entreaties that he would consider Hereford Street his home, had moved him from his fixed purpose of keeping the Alwyns at arm's length; but now a woman's voice and a woman's smile made him an unwilling captive. He could not turn and flee away. He could do nothing but remain and listen to the songs of the mermaid, whose tones rang out their sweetest and fullest for his benefit.

"I wish we could have persuaded you to come and stay with us;"—this was the burden of the melody—" papa would have taken a house at Brighton, Folkestone, Torquay—anywhere, if you had only consented to join us. We were so grievously disappointed, and, I may say for myself, so hurt——"

" Hurt, Miss Alwyn?" echoed Lawrence.

"Yes, hurt," she repeated; "no one could have grieved more than I did about the consequences my accident entailed upon you. But it was not my fault, now, was it, Mr. Barbour? —and ought you to have borne malice towards me,—ought you?"

" Malice," he said, stupified.

"I do not blame you," she went on. "I cannot tell how I myself might have felt had any such calamity befallen me; but I want us to be friends, now. I want you to believe that we regret your accident more than it is possible for you to do, and—and—I have come with papa to-day to tell you this, and to say that I, like you, have been angry—angry at your refusal to come to us; but that I am now only sorry. What a wretched thing it is never to be able to express one's meaning perfectly," finished Miss Alwyn, with engaging abruptness, leaving the disentanglement of her sentence for Lawrence.

Fill up that sentence, reader, with a by-play which was beyond all writing; with a look—with a smile—with a blush—with a drooping of the eyes—with a movement of the hands—with a peeping in and out of a dainty foot—with a tone, now of reproach, now of pathos, now of pleading; and you have the position. You have the woman who attracted Lawrence and lured him on—on, spite of his former antipathy, of his instinctive aversion.

He was but a lad. For all his wise thoughts and firm resolves, for all his manly resolution and keen perception, he was but a lad—but a reed in the hands of such as she, but as wax capable of receiving any impression she chose to stamp upon him.

Everything was in her favour—manner, appearance, dress. Shall we say dress is nothing? Shall we babble about Nature unadorned? Shall we say a pretty woman is equally pretty in any attire? Bah! There are times and places when dress is everything; when Venus herself, if she appeared with no article of attire save a piece of drapery artistically arranged, would never be asked to dance, but rather be taken forthwith in charge, and escorted to the nearest station-house. Given, a man who has not seen much of female society, and see which divinity he falls down and worships—the pure and simple, or the gorgeous and sensuous; barefooted virtue, or vice resplendent with diamonds; the lily which has toiled not, nor spun, but trusts to its own native loveliness, or the Queen of the East, clad in all manner of rich garments, and followed by a train of slaves and servants.

Which? Ah, friends, many a weary mile

humanity travels before it learns to choose the light of the home taper to that of the will-o'-the-wisp; many a heart has broken running after the end of the rainbow; many a soul has gone far astray because of the lust of the eye, which takes pleasure—and innocent enough pleasure, oftentimes, as it seems to us—in everything that the art and the skill of man have combined together to make beautiful and attractive.

This was the first moral stumbling-block that came to obstruct Lawrence Barbour's course in life. He was a slave to his senses. In his own person he disregarded luxury, he was willing and able to bear hardship and discomfort; but for all that, the fashions of this world influenced him. A handsomely furnished room, an elegantly dressed woman, a splendidly appointed equipage, an array of servants, a blaze of light, and glitter of glass, and shining of plate, produced an effect upon him all through his life which can scarcely be understood by those who have always viewed such accessories as mere matters of course—as the inevitable landscape in the background of a portrait, as the photographer's stock pillar or antique chair.

Lawrence had sense, but it was impotent against this involuntary passion. He was taken captive by his eyes, by the sweep of a dress, by the shape of a bonnet, by the arrangement of a room, by the tone of a voice. He was a slave at last; she had him to have and to hold from that day forth till the hour arrived when, bleeding and maimed, he escaped from her toils, having learnt wisdom in the only school where each man eventually becomes his own philosopher, and preaches great truths to himself out of the lesson-books of his personal experience.

She had him—she netted him with the hair he was wont to laugh at, with the eyes which had in them neither a pure nor a holy light, with the hands which were so white and treacherous, with the smile that was so sweetly cruel, with the rich attire which became her so royally —she had him, this lad, who when he grew to be a man, and entered into possession of man's estate of responsibility and sorrow, cursed the day in which he met her, the mother that bore, and the father who begat her.

Sweetly she ran on with her pleasant unisons. Strictly speaking, the music she made might not be critically correct, but Lawrence never thought of analysing it.

He wanted to hate her, and still he could not. He tried to shake off the spell she laid upon him, and think of her as the Miss Alwyn whom he and his brother were wont to mock at as she came forth from the gates of Mallingford; but the attempt was useless—he did not want to admire her, but he could not help himself; he had detested her at a distance, and now, when she spoke and smiled, he loved her.

Loved her! What a poor and feeble expression to convey an idea of the passion which took possession that day of Lawrence Barbour, and became more and more intense as the years went by, till its very fierceness worked its own destruction — till there was no more fuel left in his heart to feed the flame which had consumed his happiness.

Meanwhile, Mr. Alwyn walked from window to window, contributing his mite to the conversation, and graciously expressing his approval of the view.

"The Thames really looks exceedingly well from here," remarked the West-ender. "I had no idea there was anything so pretty on this side of London. Should not mind having a house in this neighbourhood at all; but then the want of wood is a drawback, and timber does take such a deuce of a time to grow."

Having delivered himself of which opinion, Mr. Alwyn took up another post of observation, and declared that the choice of such a residence did Mr. Sondes credit.

This sentiment reminding Miss Alwyn of the fact of Mr. Sondes' existence, she suggested the possibility to her father of their being intruders, and the consequent desirability of their immediate departure.

"Very well, my dear," acquiesced Mr. Alwyn; "just as you like. Now, Mr. Barbour, I depend on your paying us a visit; you must return a lady's call, remember; no getting off that; no escape possible, recollect; and no compromise accepted. Come to Hereford Street any day you like—only the earlier day the better, and take care of yourself, and—God bless you," which was rather a favourite form of·speech of the colonial broker, and one which always raised a doubt in Percy Forbes' mind as to the god he meant,—"whether Mammon or not," finished that incorrigible scapegrace, when alluding to the matter at a subsequent period of this story.

"And good-bye," said Miss Alwyn, in her softest tone of voice; and then Lawrence opened the drawing-room door for them to pass out, and went down the stairs, and was about to accompany them to the outer gate; but just at that juncture Olivine came shyly· forward, and beckoned him aside.

"Do not let them go, please," she said, pulling his sleeve piteously, and turning her back a little towards Miss Alwyn, who caused the child great anguish of mind by staring at her persistently.

"I have asked Nurse Mary to get dinner for them and all, and uncle will soon be home ; and he would not like them to leave. Please keep them, please do."

"Are you certain your uncle will not be angry ? " he inquired.

"Certain—sure ! " And Olivine's answer was so emphatic that Lawrence, without further hesitation, laid the state of the case before Mr. and Miss Alwyn, who, nothing loth, accepted the child's invitation, and turned back into the house, Mr. Alwyn saying, in his loftily-jocular manner,—

" Remember, little girl, if we get into trouble through this, you are to take the blame, and see us out of danger."

"Yes, sir," was Olivine's demure reply ; and then, addressing Miss Alwyn, she asked, with the quiet self-possession of an experienced hostess,—

" Would you like to come with me and take off your bonnet ? "

"Yes, I should, very much," answered Miss

Alwyn, adding, in an undertone, to her father,—

"Isn't it a perfect curiosity?"

When the bonnet had been taken off, and the shawl also—when Miss Alwyn had smoothed her hair and arranged her personal appearance generally to her liking, she happened to turn suddenly round, and caught Olivine looking her over as only children and women know how.

There was something in that look which put Miss Alwyn out, and she inquired sharply, "Well, you funny little thing, are you admiring me?" to which plain question Olivine, equally disconcerted, perhaps, returned the plain answer, "No, I am not."

CHAPTER XVII.

WHEN Mr. Sondes returned from London, he was not a little surprised to find his house in possession of the enemy, for as such he virtually regarded Mr. Alwyn. Nevertheless, war not having been openly declared, there was no resource left for him save to welcome the newcomers to his house, and bid them consider themselves at home. He was glad Olivine had played her part in the drama so discreetly; not for worlds would he have failed in any act of courtesy or hospitality.

For father and daughter to have left without eating or drinking, or taking rest, would have mortified him intensely; and accordingly he laid his hand on his little girl's head and told her she had done well, which was the more gratifying to

Olivine, as she had her own misgivings on the subject of Miss Alwyn.

But now her uncle approved of her performances, the child felt relieved and happy.

Deposed from her seat on her uncle's right hand, she still, from her corner beside Lawrence, surveyed Miss Alwyn, and made that young lady somewhat uncomfortable by reason of her scrutiny.

When Lawrence came to know Henrietta better, the beauty confessed she had undergone much at Grays by reason of Olivine.

"The little wretch made me eat in spite of myself," she said. "I felt afraid to leave any pieces, feeling those eyes were upon me," at which confession Percy Forbes, who was present, laughed delightedly.

"The East-end child seems not to have appreciated West-end fashions," he remarked, and the remark caused Miss Alwyn to flush angrily, while Lawrence answered for her, that he thought West-end fashions might do a great deal for the East-end child.

"Oh! you do, do you?" said Percy Forbes; and he laughed again, for they were all very intimate and plain-spoken in those days which had still to come, when Olivine sat on Lawrence Barbour's right hand, and kept watch over Miss Alwyn, who felt "put out" by the child's close inspection.

There are some games in which bystanders see too much of the play; there are smiles and looks, and tones and gestures, which bear a different signification to a third party to what they do to one at least of the performers. The man who guesses the secret of thimble-rigging is *de trop* between deceiver and dupe; and there is many a conjuror of whom the law takes unhappily no cognisance gliding about drawing-rooms, and putting in an appearance at evening-parties, who hates the sight of a pair of unbelieving eyes, and the curl of a contemptuous lip, when going through her paces for the benefit of some fresh victim—of some credulous simpleton.

Those were early days for Olivine to be *de trop*, and for Miss Alwyn to feel that she was so.

The social comedy, as a rule, is one not easily understood by children, and Olivine did not understand the part Miss Alwyn acted in it for many a year—oh! no, not for many a year. She only felt intuitively the same instinctive aversion to her as a dog might have done; but the young lady felt this aversion, and writhed under it.

Her prettily rounded sentences were checked at sight of Olivine's inquiring eyes; the applause which her sharp witticisms usually elicited was not sought for on this occasion, because she knew Olivine would not see the point: she had to eat, as she said, and feign no fine ladyish airs; she had to finish her wine, and allow the glass to be replenished, and utter no entreaty of " Stop, pray stop "—because she feared Olivine would lift her dark eyes and fasten them upon her wonderingly.

" What a mistake it is to have such terrible children in to dinner!" sighed Miss Alwyn, as the train dashed over the marsh lands back towards London.

"Yes. But then she is such a good little creature," answered Mr. Alwyn; "and pretty." For Mr. Alwyn was not blind, and could appreciate the making of a beautiful woman when he saw it.

"Oh dear! do you think so?" said his daughter. "She is so plain and peculiar."

"Peculiar, but not plain, Etta," replied Mr. Alwyn. "She is anything but plain; and you will allow me to be a judge on that subject, at least, I hope."

After which the judge fell asleep, and Etta continued her musings in the twilight.

Of course there is no such thing as prospective jealousy in the world; the scientific man feels no soreness when the possibility is suggested to him of that young Ozone rubbing his memory out of men's minds as the years go by; the doctor who has prescribed for all manner of ailments for forty years, invariably lays down his pen and puts his spectacles in their case, and benignly blesses the mere lad who comes to push him from his stool. It is human nature, is it not, to do so? to smile on the man or woman who is to fill up your place in the world when you have grown old, and weary, and obsolete; it is human nature to like those who are to come after you, whose feet will travel the road to success when your limbs are tottering and feeble, whose ears will listen to the throbbings of other men's hearts, when yours are deaf and treacherous; who will write books, and perform wonderful operations, and build stupendous bridges, and conquer natural difficulties, and solve still unsolved enigmas, and be sought by the learned, and titled, and wealthy, and be famous and renowned when your name, friend, when your name, high as it stands now, shall be but as a word that has been spoken, as a song that has been sung.

Is this human nature? Ah! reader, is not this rather artificial nature—conventional nature—the nature men put on when they summon up all their courage, and swear to themselves that they will not tremble when the fatal Monday comes; but go forth to meet the inevitable, calmly and decently?

Do people like being hung? do they like Jack
Ketch when they shake hands with Calcraft, or
any other of his representatives? are they perfectly resigned, think you, when they murmur
their last prayer in time before being launched
into eternity? No. Well, there is a time of
youth, and popularity, and sunshine, for most
of God's creatures, and after that the eternity
of temporal nonentity, and age, and winter
gloom.

But the children and the lovers, and the
beginners and the strugglers, are bathed in the
sunshine still, and the most that those whose
day has gone by can do, is to sit down re-
signedly by the quiet hearth and thank God
for the glory which once lighted up their path,
though the glory and the brightness have
departed.

And the application of all this? you ask.
The application is, that although Miss Alwyn's
feelings towards Olivine Sondes were not amiable,
still they were natural. The one success in life
which a beautiful woman can achieve she saw

prospectively achieved after she was *passé* by another. Prospectively she was jealous — the present beauty of the future belle—of the loveliness which was coming—of the grace that was to charm.

Instinctively, as Olivine disliked her, so she disliked Olivine—disliked her from the moment the child answered her question, as to whether she were admiring her, with the words, " No, I am not."

That was the glove thrown down—that was the challenge to battle, and nothing Olivine essayed could take the sting out of that sentence.

All in vain she tried to amuse Miss Alwyn after dinner; brought her books, exhibited her pets, took her round the garden, gathered her a bouquet, and did her childish best to make the rich man's daughter comfortable.

All in vain. Miss Alwyn closed the books, buried her nose in the flowers, and then said their perfume was overpowering; the terrier would not make friends, and she merely smiled listlessly at the begging cat; while she teased the parrot till he bit her; whereupon the young lady screamed aloud, and declared that so dangerous an animal ought not to be kept.

"Why did you not tell me he would bite, you stupid child?" exclaimed Miss Alwyn, red with anger and pain.

"I did not know, ma'am; I did not—I did not, indeed!" Olivine pleaded. "He never bit me."

"Of course not. What is there about you to make him do anything of the kind? You never excite him nor tease him. Horrid wretch! I wonder somebody does not twist his neck. I am sure I should if I were in the house."

"I don't think you would," said Olivine, quietly.

"Don't you, indeed, Miss Wisdom? What should prevent me?"

"I would," answered the child, and her breath came quick and short as she spoke the words. "You should not touch my parrot—no, not unless you killed me first."

Whereupon Miss Alwyn burst out laughing.

"What a little tragedy queen it is," she said; "how its cheeks flame and its hands clench, and its eyes sparkle at the idea of the combat. Come to me, Olivine," she finished; "I was only in fun; I would not touch your parrot, child. Now, tell me all about yourself, and how you contrive to spend the days."

Very doubtfully Olivine accepted this apology; with still greater doubt she replied to all demands on her confidence; but yet, having nothing to conceal, she told how she amused herself and Lawrence; how he used to sing to her and tell her stories, and how sometimes he told her stories still.

There was not a detail of their daily life but was extracted from Olivine in due course by the lady whom she did not admire, and who left the flowers the child had so carefully gathered for her behind on the table; while she carried away, with a smile and a coquettish affectation, a few buds Lawrence selected and arranged with trembling hands, and presented to her with a certain boyish grace as a souvenir of her visit to Grays.

“As though I were likely to forget it?” she said, from her seat in the railway-carriage; and then their fingers somehow locked together in another good-bye; and though the light was fading, Lawrence could see that she blushed violently.

Another moment, and the guard banged-to the door, the whistle sounded, and the visitors were off.

Home through the twilight walked the youth, feeling dizzy as if he had drunk too much wine, and yet seeming to tread on air; home to think of her, to dream of her, to feel all his old acquaintances and pursuits insupportable, to ask himself what it all meant, what glamour she had cast over him.

When he reached Mr. Sondes’ house, Olivine and her uncle were seated together in the drawing-room looking out upon the Thames and the surrounding country that lay bathed in the light of a young moon.

“You saw them off, Lawrence?” Mr. Sondes said, interrogatively.

"Yes, sir," was the reply; "and I promised Mr. Alwyn I would dine with them on Friday next, even if you could not get off your engagement."

"Quite right, my boy. It is you they want, not me," answered Mr. Sondes. "On the whole, that adventure of yours is not going to turn out such a misfortune as I once thought it would."

"I do not know what you mean," Lawrence said; and immediately Mr. Sondes laughed, and answered,—

"Ah well! you will know what I mean some day, without any further explanation," and he laughed again; but Lawrence did not feel pleased for all that, and sat down and looked out at the moonlight, marvelling.

"I think you are wrong about Mr. Alwyn," he ventured, after a pause. "He said to me, over and over again, that he did wish you to come very much. He is most anxious to know more of you."

"Think of that!" exclaimed Mr. Sondes, meditatively; "and I have done business with him these twenty years, without ever having an idea of anything of the kind."

"And we lived beside him for nearly four years," returned Lawrence, "and were never asked inside his door. But I am not going to bear malice on that account," went on the youth magnanimously; "a man has a right to choose his acquaintances for himself at any time of his life."

"Certainly," acquiesced Mr. Sondes; "and a man has a right to decline making acquaintances at any time of his life"—which, being an incontrovertible truth, Lawrence abstained from any reply likely to force its application to the case in point.

"It is decidedly a good thing for you," said Mr. Sondes, after a pause. "Mr. Alwyn can push you on in the world if he likes. He can give you a good berth and a good salary to-morrow, and initiate you into the mysteries of his business the day after. If you continue to visit at Hereford Street you will mix much in society and see a good deal of the world. You will form acquaintances such as you could never hope to meet with in Stepney; and altogether it will be 'your own fault, I should say, if you do not make your fortune somehow or other out of the affair."

"Make my fortune with a constitution not worth that!" and Lawrence, as he spoke, held out his hand full of leaves he had been nervously pulling off one of the flowers out of poor Olivine's rejected bouquet—"not worth that!"

"Tut, man!" retorted Mr. Sondes. "What a fuss you are in about your ribs! If every bone in your body were broken, you could not make yourself out a greater cripple. You will be strong enough some day; and, meantime, it is a great matter you have found a backer like Mr. Alwyn, able and willing to give you a lift."

There was silence for a few minutes, then Lawrence spoke,—

"Mr. Sondes," he began, "I wish you would not misunderstand me in this business. I wish you would believe I am in earnest when I say that no offer Mr. Alwyn could make would induce me to leave you and Mr. Perkins, so long as you are both willing to keep me. There is no unselfishness in this," he continued hurriedly, seeing Mr. Sondes was about to reply. "None; I could not bear to owe anything to Mr. Alwyn, either to his kindness, his generosity, or his justice; and if you think in accepting his invitation and going to his house I lay myself under an obligation of any kind, I will not go. I place myself in your hands: I will go, or I will stay, according as you answer," and Lawrence leaned forward across the window, and sat with the bright moonlight streaming full upon him, waiting for Mr. Sondes' reply.

But Mr. Sondes did not reply. He turned towards Olivine and said,—

"It is high time you were in bed, little one. You ought to have been asleep an hour ago. Run away now, my pet. Good night, Olivine, good night:" He put the hair back from her brow and kissed her, then he took her head between his two hands and turned it towards the window, and looked at the child with such

an expression of love in his face as Lawrence
had never seen upon any face before.

Afterwards he kissed her once again, and bade
her depart. But before she obeyed, she went up
to Lawrence, who, according to his custom, kissed
her also whilst he bade her good night.

Up to that time, Mr. Sondes had taken no
notice of this polite attention on Lawrence's
part, or, if he did, had passed it over as something not worth thinking about; but on the occasion in question a troubled look came into his
eyes, and an idea into his mind that he was not
the very first person who had unconsciously built
castles only to see them levelled with the ground.

Even while Olivine was closing the door
behind her, he had made up his mind as to his
future course; and then he threw himself back
in his chair, and gazing out at the Thames and
the lowlands lying down by the shore, and the
Kentish hills across the river, rather than at
Lawrence, answered the young man's question
thus,—

" If I had a son of my own come to your time

of life, I should reply to him just as I am going to reply to you now. Take all I am about to say for what you think it is worth. My opinion is, that in going to Hereford Street you place yourself under no obligation, but you put yourself in danger."

"In danger," repeated Lawrence; "I do not exactly——"

"I was about to explain," interrupted Mr. Sondes. "Miss Alwyn is a very handsome young lady; probably you never knew how handsome till to-day, and you may have happened to gather out of the course of your reading, Lawrence, that men will be men, and fall in love with pretty women, let the after-cost of that pleasure prove what it may. Now suppose you fall in love with Miss Alwyn."

Here Mr. Sondes paused; but Lawrence made no observation. He seemed to have gone inside himself for the time being, and sat there with his hands clasped tightly together, silent and listening.

"Suppose you fall in love with Miss Alwyn,"

continued Mr. Sondes, "you will surely be preparing a great disappointment for yourself; she is certain to marry wealth. That is a game in which I fear all the moves would be against you; for she will lead you on, step by step; she is just the woman to do it for her own vanity's sake; and then, when she has got your heart, she will cast it away. I am told that was what she did with Mr. Forbes."

"Percy Forbes!" exclaimed Lawrence. "The man never had a heart either to give or be cast away."

"Perhaps so, perhaps not," was the cool reply; "in any case, I have said my say. Now decide for yourself, go or remain away; accept or decline; only remember my words, the girl is not a straightforward honest girl, and she will not develop into an honest, straightforward woman. She has too much manner, she is full of compliment and address, she would like to have everybody at her feet, ay, even an old fellow like myself; she is not the sort of daughter-in-law I should care to welcome home had I a son.

But there, I have done. Do not answer me; do not think me prejudiced and unkind, only think over my words. And God bless you, lad, and God keep you, for you have the voyage still to make, and cannot know where the quicksands lie on which so many a gallant ship has foundered."

With that Mr. Sondes arose, and held out his hand to Lawrence, who took it gratefully.

For an instant he hesitated whether he should not follow Mr. Sondes' implied advice, and keep away from Hereford Street. Pride, consistency, caution, all bade him turn a dea. ear to the blandishments of the parvenu's daughter.

Should he visit at the house he had vowed never to enter; should he be indebted to Mr. Alwyn for so much as a single dinner; should he throw himself in the way of incurring expenses he could ill afford; of acquiring tastes he had no means of gratifying? He would flee the temptation. He decided he would, and he opened his lips to say so; but then a vision of Miss Alwyn, as he had seen her that day, in her perfect feminine attire, with her seductive smiles, appeared unto him once more, and Lawrence was lost!

"I will think it over," he said; and the strange calmness of his tone struck Mr. Sondes as peculiar. "I will think it over; and, meantime, thank you."

Having uttered which speech, Lawrence went up to his own bed-chamber on the upper story, and there the storm broke out.

"Danger!" he thought. "Danger from her —from the girl I have laughed at. Fall in love with her, indeed! A good idea." And he tried to feel amused, but failed. "I don't believe she is the same," he continued. "There must be two sisters, or cousins, or something; that cannot be the girl who used to ride out with her groom close beside her every day. Marry wealth, will she? We shall see. I suppose that is a race where horses of all colours may enter! Not honest and straightforward! The man must have taken a few glasses too much wine. Would like to net him. No such difficult matter, I should say," and Lawrence, standing by the upper window, looked out over the landscape, and thought of her with just that passionate intensity which such a nature was certain to feel for the first woman who had touched his boyish heart, who had captivated his boyish fancy.

Next morning he said to Mr. Sondes,—

"I think I had better go to Hereford Street; it would seem rude and ungracious not to do so; and besides, I promised to go—that is, if it will make no difference between us."

"Difference! not the least in the world. I will always do what I can for you. That is the way," soliloquised Mr. Sondes, as the youth left the room;—"that is the way with all of you. If God sends a woman into the world, you avoid her as you might a pestilence; but let the devil furnish society with a first-rate article out of his own department, and men break their necks running after her sinnership. So, Master Lawrence Barbour—this is the result of our chemical experiments, of our walks, and talks, and various readings. It is all for the best, no doubt. So I must e'en build my castle elsewhere."

And the first castle Mr. Soudes set about erecting after this was a country house near Chingford in Essex, to which cheerful abode he consigned Olivine, and an elderly governess, seeing her of necessity so seldom that the child's heart was almost broken, and her health and spirits began to fail. Then the man repented him of his rashness, and took the little girl home once again to the old mansion in Stepney, where Lawrence Barbour hardly ever came in those days, to sing songs to cheer her loneliness, to repeat stories to fill her imagination and satisfy her heart.

Lawrence had by this time discovered a much more excellent way of spending his life than devoting his leisure to the entertainment and instruction of "such a baby as Olivine." While he worked, he worked, as Mr. Perkins said, like "a Briton;" when he idled, he exchanged his office drudgery for but another kind of labour.

Had the London streets been a treadmill, he could not more regularly have traversed them.

West, due West, every moment he could spare, to Hereford Street. West, due West, carefully dressed and with an eager anxious face, he sallied out continually in the evenings, to concert, or theatre, or opera, or any place where he had a chance of meeting her; while Mrs. Perkins, watching his departure from kitchen or parlour, was wont to remark with a sound which seemed something between a sigh and a sneer and a groan:

"There he goes again,—there he goes."

CHAPTER XVIII.

SNARED.

At about this period of my story, Mrs. Perkins considered it her duty greatly to inconvenience the household at Distaff Yard, by first turning every room out of window, and then presenting for the consideration of those interested and uninterested in the subject, a creature which had always been Lawrence's especial horror, a baby.

The house-cleaning, Mrs. Perkins kindly explained to Lawrence, she superintended in person, and assisted in at various times, because "nobody knows what may happen, and I should not like poor Josiah to think I left everything in a muddle behind me."

"Hang it all," retorted poor Josiah on one occasion (only his phraseology was stronger), "if I had my choice in the matter, I would rather you left things in a muddle, than keep us now in such a devil of a mess;" whereupon Mrs. Perkins said he had not the heart of a man, and declared he never would know her value till she was laid out, and he a-wearing a black 'at-band for her,—"if you would even do that much out of respect," finished Mrs. Perkins with a burst of tears, that, as it seemed to Lawrence might have continued flowing for ever, had her attention not been distracted from her wrongs, to her rights by Ada, who, having at the beginning of the conference, stuffed her entire hand into her mouth, now sat in a corner rocking herself backwards and forwards, and giggling as though some capital joke were being enjoyed by those present.

"You'll do that again, will you, miss?" exclaimed Mrs. Perkins, administering such a series of slaps to Miss Ada's bare neck, that her shoulders resembled, after the operation, nothing so much as a piece of very inferior and undesirable raw beef. "You'll do that again! laugh at your own mother, and sit idling there, instead of being at your book or your sampler. It is a step-mamma you want over you,—that is what it is, and that is what you may have before you are many weeks older, let me tell you——"

At the contemplation of this appalling picture, Ada's courage succumbed, and she gave way to the most frightful shrieks imaginable—shrieks, however, that were in due time eclipsed by the new-comer, which lifted up its voice and wept in vain remonstrance at having been born into the world in general and into Distaff Yard in particular.

Lawrence was rather amusing over that baby in the drawing-room at Hereford Street. To do him strict justice, he did not hold his cousin's ménage up to ridicule, or call Mr. Perkins' children by opprobrious names in the select regions of the West; but the baby was common ground. Any baby, everybody's baby, the little circle unanimously decided was fair game. A baby could not be considered so much the part of any special family as a unit of the great nation of babies.

"They all look the same—they all cry the same—they are all worshipped the same! Anything else, Percy?" finished Miss Alwyn.

"No, thank heaven; my experience of the creatures has not been sufficiently extensive to enable me to describe their peculiarities," answered Mr. Forbes. "We must yield the palm in that respect to Mr. Barbour. He is grand, I consider, on the subject. Now, Mr. Barbour." And thereupon Mr. Barbour entered into a long description of the state of the household, which was in some respects a pure democracy, in others an absolute despotism, "with poor Mr. Perkins as meek as a lamb, and the baby a raging lion." He told of the tin saucepans, filled with unutterable compounds, in the parlour—of Mr. Perkins' resignation—of the rejoicings of various visitors—of an elderly and fat individual, who seemed to think she deserved well of heaven and her

country for having assisted at so many ceremonies of a similar nature.

"She and I are at daggers drawn," continued
Lawrence, " because I cursed the baby—screech-
ing little wretch! It is no joke turning into
bed at twelve and turning out regularly at six,
and having one's night's rest destroyed by a continuous wail. She said the worst wish she
wished me was that I might never have one,
and I answered that I hoped to heaven I never
should, at any rate not within hearing distance;
whereupon she observed—' Bless its little 'art, a
precious lamb;' and I remarked, 'Hum! not—
bless—its little throat for a yelling imp!'"

"Why do you not come and stay here?"
inquired Mr. Alwyn, one day as he sat at
dessert.

"And have to leave at four in the morning,
to get to Limehouse at six?" answered Lawrence.

"Why not cut Limehouse altogether; why not
try for a situation in the City?"

"Because I am learning a good trade where I

have cast my lot, because the business suits me and I suit the business, because I never shall be able to sit at a desk, because chemistry is precisely the occupation I like best," was the reply.

"And because chemistry as practised in Distaff Yard is so peculiarly respectable," remarked Mr. Alwyn.

"We are honest in our dishonesty in Distaff Yard," retorted Lawrence, "which is more than many first-class City firms could assert,"—at which home-thrust Mr. Alwyn felt a little nettled, and answered,—

"That is one of Mr. Sondes' opinions. It is a pity for a young man to adopt ideas second-hand."

"If the cut of my coat chance to resemble Mr. Sondes', that is no reason why I should be accused of borrowing it from him," said Lawrence hotly. "I have gone in for chemistry, Mr. Alwyn, and I mean to stick to it, and I intend to make my fortune out of it. I suppose there is money to be made from other articles on earth besides West India produce."

"Take another glass of wine, Mr. Barbour," was Mr. Alwyn's reply; and Lawrence took the hint as well as the wine, and let the discussion drop.

He would not allow the rich man to help him up. He accepted his hospitality, but that was all; for money, or assistance of any kind, he never was indebted to the owner of Mallingford; nay, more, when he went down to Hertfordshire, eighteen months after his first arrival in London, he would not stay with the Alwyns, preferring rather the meagre hospitality of the Clay Farm, and the somewhat solitary state of Lallard House, to a week's sojourn in his old home.

In his outward man he was much improved by his residence in the great city. Without any of the personal advantages nature had lavished so freely on Percy Forbes, he was yet sufficiently good-looking and gentlemanlike to pass muster in any society. There was something in his appearance also which attracted attention, something in the peculiar expression of his eyes, in the firm, hard set of his face, which was old beyond his years;

in the decision of his manner; in the courage,
not to say occasional brusqueness of his replies.

The world has a respect, as a rule, for those
who are not afraid to contradict its maxims.
It is apt to attribute to cleverness expressions
which oftentimes spring merely from a positive
and self-reliant temper. Women especially took
kindly to the young man, and tried hard to lure
him from the allegiances of his existence ; but in
vain. To business and the East End he devoted his working-hours ; to Hereford Street
and Henrietta Alwyn he gave up every leisure
moment.

Not but that he fought against himself and
her ; not that she ever had him in such subjec-
tion as her other admirers. He would stand in
his own room after he returned from one of
the Hereford Street parties, and swear by everything holy and by everything evil that Henrietta
Alwyn's reign over him should have an end, that
he would go no more to her father's, that the
acquaintance should cease ; and once, I think,
he might have held fast to his purpose, had not

Percy Forbes said to him as they walked together down Brook Street the following night :—

"Look here, Barbour. I know you do not like me, and I know you do not trust me, but I want to say something to you for all that. Don't get too fond of Miss Alwyn; she will only fool you as she has fooled others; and even if she were willing to marry you, no worse luck could happen. I have been through the fire there, and know all about her from bitter experience."

"And it is manly for you to speak about Miss Alwyn as you are doing, I suppose," was the reply.

"It is friendly, at all events," answered Percy coolly, as they parted, the one to make his way into Piccadilly, and the other to walk back slowly and thoughtfully on his way to Limehouse.

He would not give her up, he would believe no falsehoods about her, he would work, he would learn, he would make a name, and a fortune, and a position, and lay all at her feet, only praying her to take him along with them.

He felt sure, he felt as positive as he was

iving that Miss Alwyn loved him; she might have fooled others, she might have flirted with others, she might have rejected others, but she should not refuse him, she should not.

And then he cursed his destiny which prevented his asking her to marry him at once. Poor as he still was, he could not run the risk of being thought mercenary; and so he hung back, growing shyer and shyer as the weeks and the months went by, while she became kinder and more gracious every day, making more evident advances as he receded, and filling his life full of sunshine, gilding his work with a glory of love and hope, and causing the hours to flit by on the wings of joy and happiness.

He was too sure of her; he never heeded the voice which whispered caution in his ear. In spite of all advice, notwithstanding his own misgivings, forgetful of his former prejudices, he had set himself on a course in which he was determined to continue spite of wind or weather. As Jacob served Laban for Rachel, so Lawrence Barbour served mammon for Henrietta Alwyn, for the girl whom in his inmost heart he despised himself for loving, whom he knew to be ill-tempered, hypocritical, unfeeling, cruel; but at the same time beautiful and fascinating exceedingly. Her beauty was the bait that allured him; he had still to learn fully the strength and sharpness of the hook which that bait concealed.

CHAPTER XIX.

A LITTLE GOSSIP.

THERE is probably no place on earth where so much work is got through as in London; where so much thought, so much "doing," so much feeling, so much hearing, so much seeing, is compressed into the days as in this, the great city of labour.

Here, men live out their threescore years and ten before they reach middle age. Event succeeds to event; duty to duty; employment to employment, without pause or break: over the stones, and along the pavement, the tide of existence rolls without cessation; through men's brains there is a great thoroughfare worn by the traffic of work—work always beginning, never ending; in their ears is a continual noise, caused by the present wheels of something that has to be done to-day, and a dull roar, announcing the coming something which must be done to-morrow, and the morrow after, and through every succeeding morrow of their lives.

Here can be no folding together of the hands, till the hour comes for final rest. Here can be no slippered ease, no dreamy contemplation; every soldier of the great army is on duty, if he comes even within sight of the battle-field; work stands on the doorstep waiting to be attended to; work waits for audience in the innermost chamber; work takes its seat in brougham and barouche, and who shall say it nay; work lurks beside the sleeper, and wakes him through the night, lest even in dreams he should forget its sovereignty, forget this Pharaoh of the modern Egypt, who answers the appeal of his slaves, however weary or however worn they may be, with the taunting sentence, "Make brick, make brick; ye are idle, ye are idle."

Work!—every man's mind is full of it. See

you, as you walk along the streets in the early morning, men hurrying city-ward, men going forth to their labours.

The pavements are crowded; the omnibuses are laden; there are carriages proceeding eastward; there are cabs following close after one another.

Whichever quarter you take, North, East, South, or West, it is the same—over London Bridge they come, seventeen conveyances a minute; down the City Road and Shoreditch, down Goswell and St. John Streets, pour the inhabitants of Holloway and Highbury, of Islington, of Pentonville, of Hackney, of Bethnal Green, of Kingsland, Dalston, Cambridge Heath, Hoxton and Homerton, and Barnsbury and Ball's Pond; along the Commercial and Mile End Roads troop the dwellers in Stepney, Bow, Limehouse, Shadwell, Poplar, Whitechapel, and Wapping. Down Holborn and through the Strand sweeps the West End tide, bearing with it the denizens of Kensington and Bayswater, of Notting Hill, of St. John's Wood, of Paddington, Tyburnia, Belgravia, Pimlico, Chelsea, Hammersmith, and Fulham. As for the South—across the bridges it sends its tributaries to the great human stream. By train, by omnibus, on foot, they come to swell the flood: from Greenwich and Blackheath, from New Cross, Peckham, Lewisham, Camberwell, Sydenham, Norwood, Walworth, Brixton, Bermondsey, Deptford, Kennington, Lambeth, Clapham, Battersea, Vauxhall, and all outlying towns and villages they come to work; they are to be met with in the back streets as in the main thoroughfares; they are to be found taking short cuts on foot,—beheld in the regular roads seated on the tops of omnibuses, or hurrying from the various railway termini.

It matters little in which direction the reader turns his steps, whether he elect to make his observations in Aldgate or the Borough, in Stangate or the Horseferry Road, at the Canal Bridge in Clerkenwell, or any remoter locality, the result will be the same. Every house contributes its unit to the great congregation; from each dwelling some one goes "forth to his work and his labour till the evening."

And this work, this constant labour, stamps a certain character on the faces of the Londoners, which is to be observed on the faces of none of their countrymen. They seem to be always looking after something which is a long way in advance of them, thinking of something in which the busy streets and the passers-by have no part or share.

There is a most extraordinary look in the countenance of a Londoner, when he is "himself," when he does not know any one is observing him, when he is not talking or acting any social part. He appears like one who sees without observing, who hears without noticing, who thinks without analysing, who, living continually in the midst of his fellows, is still mentally alone, who is only vaguely conscious of the existence of that second life, which to philosophers seems the real life, and who is amazed, and grateful, and yet half-afraid when some one puts his thoughts into words for him, separates the floating mass of aspirations and regrets, and hopes and sorrows, and feelings which are common to us all, and presents each crystallised into its own proper form, clothed with its own especial beauty, whether that beauty be sad or bright, for his contemplation.

The very walk of these workers is different from the walk of the semi-workers elsewhere.

Take your stand, reader, any morning at the top of Cheapside, and you will understand what I mean.

The country people move along swiftly, or slowly, as the case may be; but in either case indefinitely. The Londoners, on the contrary, walk as men having a purpose, straight on to their object.

Distances in the great city may have some share in producing this result: when a man has but to lounge down the street, or round the corner—when he has but to stretch out his hand and lay it on the shoulder of John, Tom, and Harry—when he can take his time over his meals—when there is no hurry about any-thing, naturally, his walk becomes desultory and leisurely, like his business. The men and the

women around him take the world, its labours,
its pleasures, its sorrows quietly. The pace of
life is not the same over the fields as over the
stones. Every person in the remote regions
where the country people come from, has less to
do in existence than it is possible for him to get
through. Let the Londoner work as hard as he
will, he still finds there is more to be done than
he can quite accomplish. When he wakes in the
morning, it is with no vague feeling of wonder as
to what may turn up for him to do; he knows
enough is left from the previous day to occupy
all his time; it is a race with him from the
cradle to the grave; not always a Race for
Wealth, friends, but oftentimes, alas! a Race for
Bread.

Striving, fighting, working; always busy; never
idle; meeting with competition at every turn;
having his wits daily sharpened by necessity and
experience, the Londoner becomes superficially
clever, and preternaturally active. Farther, he
never knows of his own knowledge the meaning
of the word "ennui;" the day is never too long

for him—not even the twenty-first of June has hours enough in it for the arrears to be got under—the balance to be accurately struck.

The days are moments, the years months; and it was with the intensest surprise that Lawrence Barbour, counting up the length of his sojourn in London, found he had passed four summers there; four summers and four winters, and that it was February again, and the anniversary of his coming to the great Babylon once more.

For the years had passed like a watch in the night. Looking back, he could not realise to himself that the time had come, and the time had gone, so rapidly; he could scarcely believe he had entered London a boy, and that he was now a man; and yet in those four years he had lived longer than during the score passed previously in the country.

He was still in Mr. Perkins' employment, though not an inmate of Mr. Perkins' house; further contributions to the domestic establishment on the part of Mrs. Perkins, rendering such an arrangement as inconvenient to the chemist, as distasteful to his kinsman.

From the back bed-room, from a perfect opera of juvenile woes, from the society of "the mother of a family," from the contemplation of Ada's hair, from meals graced by the presence of the entire household—a baby in arms included—from tin saucepans, and horsehair chairs,—behold Lawrence translated to "apartments,"—to three rooms in a house, concerning which I shall have more to say hereafter,—to furniture of his own, to tea and coffee that he made for himself, to dinners and suppers which he ordered on his own responsibility.

This change had come about on the occasion of one of those events when the assistance of Lawrence's natural enemy was considered necessary.

As it never seemed to enter into Mr. Perkins' head that his house required enlarging, Lawrence took it upon him to hint that the family needed reducing; and although both Mr. and Mrs. Perkins urged him to remain, remarking that they could manage "somehow," the young man steeled himself against all entreaties, and moved into the apartments of which honourable mention has already been made.

"It is preparatory to his getting married, my dear," was Mrs. Jackson's comment on the affair, to which Mrs. Perkins on her first day of receiving visitors groaned out a resolute dissent.

"Do you think Miss Alwyn would come and live *there* ?" she asked. "No, not if she was in love with him fifty times over, and him twice as sweet on her as he is."

"I did not say he was going to bring her to Mrs. Pratting's first floor," answered Mrs. Jackson. "I only said it looked like getting married, and so it does. If not marriage, what else ? What would a young man like him investigate in furniture for, if not with a view of settling ? With my own two eyes I saw his rooms yesterday, and more beautiful rooms, I will say, could not be found in Limehouse. He has a piano, and a couple of easy-chairs, and a carpet all moss and green leaves, and hangings

of damask—worsted damask, for I felt it with
my bare hand—and a round table, and a chiffon-
nière with a lot of gimcracks on it, not decanters,
and cut tumblers, and such useful things as we
have on our sideboard,—but glass 'gobbelets,'
I think Mrs. Pratting called them, that looked
big enough, but that weren't a feather-weight in
your hand when you lifted them,—and a large
china vase, like what you would see in a grocer's
window, and gilt flower-holders that were mighty
fine and pretty,—and a naked woman riding on a
lion, and a couple of other figures without a
stitch on them,—not a blessed rag more than
that baby wore when it came into the world,
—which I thought were barely decent, and that
I know I would bundle out of the window
pretty sharp if Samuel brought them home to
me,—and the arm-chairs were covered with
velvet—real Geneva velvet, Mrs. Pratting assured
me,—and he has got a clock on the mantel-shelf,
with two more naked boys sprawling on it, and
spill-boxes, and lustres, and cigar-cases, and,—
my dear, you must go and see it for yourself."

" And, oh ! I forgot to tell you," she continued, without giving Mr. Perkins time to answer, " over the piano there is a linengraph of a young lady that is as like Miss Alwyn, Mrs. Pratting tells me, as two peas."

" ' And well, Mrs Pratting,' says I, ' if so be as how Miss Alwyn is like that, she is like a disreputable baggage, which is all the remark I have got to make on the subject.'

" With that, you'd a' thought she was going to jump out of her skin with fear; and ' Hush, hush, ma'am, if you please, for there is some people as lives in this house, and pays their rent regular week by week, and the tradespeople honourable, as has got two pair of ears, and half a dozen sets of eyes, and I won't mention no names for fear of accidents ; ' to which I made answer that we were in a free country, and all equals in the sight of God; and that, if he had left any of his ears or eyes behind him, he was welcome to my opinions about the young woman in the chemise.

" ' He can't send you to Newgate, Mrs. Pratting,'

I wound up with, 'for anything I say; and if he was here himself, I would say just the same to him.'

" ' But if he knew I had showed you the rooms, he would be so angry.'

"' Would he?' sàys I. ' Well, I never was backward in showing him mine, nor making him welcome to a cup of tea, or a glass of hot brandy and water, which, I will do him the justice to say, he was not above accepting; and, if it was not that you are a lone woman, Mrs. Pratting, and that the rent is, perhaps, as you say, an object, I would be downright angry with you for making such a fuss over Mr. Lawrence Barbour, who is no better nor a servant, so to speak; and is not even on his own account, nor a householder like yourself, Mrs. Pratting.' "

I wish it were possible for me to sketch Mrs. Perkins and Mrs. Jackson as they looked to an outsider, while the soap-boiler's wife thus gossiped over my hero's affairs. If it might be that each reader could see the pair for himself, how far superior would such a sight prove than any description put into any form of words ? The only time in her existence, perhaps, when Mrs. Perkins looked even passable, was on those not rare occasions on which she was "at home'" in her bedroom, and "received" in a dressing-gown and night-cap. The absence of colours—dingy or gay—was an immense improvement to her appearance; and the consciousness that she had done her duty, and fulfilled her mission, imparted a certain dignity to her general deportment which was a desirable change from her usual fussy manner.

Further, she had her own peculiar ideas of etiquette, and a portion of this etiquette consisted in having a Bible and Prayer-book constantly beside her. Regularly as a baby arrived on the scene, that Bible and Prayer-book were produced. They came out with the white dimity; when the chintz hangings were taken down, and the snowy curtains put up, the orthodox volumes were disinterred from their own especial corner in Mrs. Perkins' fancy drawer, which contained her sleeves, collars, ribbon-bows, Sunday brooch, and such like, and laid on the table beside the bed, not for use, but for ornament.

They were put there, Lawrence always thought, for the same purpose as some captains carry a "caul" to sea with them, as charms against danger. They were both full of markers, made of perforated cardboard, with texts embroidered on some, while others bore such mundane sen·tences of affection and entreaty, as "For Susannah Anne," "Remember me!" "Dinna Forget!" "I love thee!" "Near to my heart!" the heart being worked in blue and red and green floss silk, in that uncomfortable shape which hearts are popularly supposed to resemble, with a border of shamrocks, or roses, or fancy leaves, running round the edge."

These books had a subduing effect on Mrs. Perkins, the same as standing in a cathedral produces on many persons, and the nurse induced a still greater quietude of address; the chemist's wife always felt, as she phrased it, "quite the lady," when she was being looked after and attended to, having nothing to think of, as Lawrence's natural enemy declared, but herself, and nothing to do but " take her victuals reg'lar," a part of the performance which, it may incidentally be remarked, the nurse by no means neglected on her own account.

Altogether, those were very happy days in Mrs. Perkins' estimation ; and, as she assured Mrs. Jackson, it gave her real pleasure to see " a friend as was a friend," we may assume that gossip was better than " victuals " to her.

There, at any rate, she sate beside the fire, well propped up with unnecessary pillows, and almost smothered in an enormous arm-chair ; Bible and Prayer-book at her right hand, the inevitable towel-horse, covered with clothes that never seem to get aired in the houses of managing women, usurping all the heat,—Mrs. Jackson on the further side of the hearth, and the nurse flitting in and out, and attending to baby, and insisting on the mother swallowing any and every mess it entered into her diabolical old head to concoct in the lower regions.

But when the talk came round to Lawrence Barbour, nurse found that baby required more than ordinary attention, and kindly stayed in the room and joined in the conversation.

"Mr. Barbour is a young gentleman as'll never come to no good," she remarked, from the other side of the bed; whereupon Mrs. Perkins, fortified by the presence of the sacred volume, hoped Mrs. Nettlefield would remember what her Bible taught her, and have " respect to persons," which quotation (being in no position to dispute its accuracy) the nurse received as *bonâ fide*, merely observing that she did not think Mr. Barbour was one of those young men as the Scriptures meant she ought to respect.

"And whether they do or not, I shan't," finished the woman, rolling the unfortunate baby —of which at the time she held possession—over and over like a wheel as she spoke.

"I wonder where he gets the money ? " said Mrs. Perkins, after a pause.

" Likely as not gambling ; for there's nothing I would put past him," answered the voice which seemed one too many during the conversation.

"I was not addressing you, Mrs. Nettlefield," observed Mrs. Perkins, with dignity.

"And I was not a-dressing of you, ma'am," was the reply, "but of this precious child;" which answer seemed the more aggravating as Mrs. Nettlefield understood Mrs. Perkins' meaning perfectly. And it is not very pleasant, when a woman does adventure on a dignified form of speech, to have it flung back in her face with scorn and ridicule.

"You ought not to forget, nurse," interposed Mrs. Jackson at this juncture, "that the young gentleman we are a speaking of is a near relation to Mr. Perkins.

"I never said Mr. Perkins could help his relations," retorted Mrs. Nettlefield; "but what I do say, and what I will say, is, that a young man who could go on as I have heard Mr. Barbour a-going on with my own two ears, is not fit to be in any respectable house, but ought to 'sociate with them statutes and images and

baggages you yourself, Mrs. Jackson, was a-
talking about five minutes ago. The like of
him,"—and at this stage of the proceedings she
laid the infant flat on its back, in order to devote
herself more entirely to the subject in hand—
"I never did hear, though I have heard some
men, too, talking again children in my life. When
'Erbert was born, I am sure it has made my
flesh creep like worms just to listen to him. He
never spoke of that sweet lamb except as 'the
devil,' and he were always asking of me to stuff
a wet towel down its throat, and inquiring if
there was not a grate in the house big enough to
hold it. I declare he used to scare me, coming
out of his room in the middle of the night, when
I were a-going down into the kitchen to get
a cup of tea for you, ma'am, coming out half-
dressed, and with that shock of hair tumbled all
over his head. 'For the love of 'eaven, Mrs.
Nettlefield,' he would say, 'do gag the devil;'
and he would stand there, and curse in the dark
night till he had me all of a tremble. And
then he would ask me, if I would not give him

sleep, to give him at any rate a drop of my gin—
as if gin was a thing I accustomed myself to !
and I could hear him laughing to himself when
he went back to his bed. Many a time I wondered no judgment fell on him."

"Well, we can only speak about people as we
finds them," answered Mrs. Perkins. "And
though he may not have made himself agreeable
to you, Mrs. Nettlefield, I must say he was
always most genteel and affable to me. It is
trying, if you come to think of it, for anybody
not a mother to be wakened out of his first sleep
—and it was not too much he had in those days ;
and you can't expect a boy, as one may say he
was then, to have the feelings of the father of a
family. For my part, I always did like him, and
I always shall." Whereupon Mrs. Jackson expressed her opinion that it was a pity "he had
fell in, as he had, getting extravagant notions,
and tastes above his class."

At that Mrs. Perkins fired up.

"Let me tell you, Mrs. Jackson," she said,
"as how the Barbours of Mallingford used to

associate along with the nobility; and as for the Alwyns being above Lawrence Barbour in station, they are no such thing: Mr. Sondes himself says so, and you will allow him to be a judge, I hope. And to this day, when he goes to his native place, he always stays a few days with my Lord Lallard, which I saw one day at St. George's, and a plainer, pleasanter spoken man I would not wish to meet with. 'Will you come home with me, little girl,' he says to Ada; and I thought to myself at the time, poor man, he'd be glad to have one like her; for I am given to understand they have neither chick nor child. So as I was a-saying of, Mrs. Jackson, it is no rise in the world for Lawrence to be thick with the Alwyns, for he comes of good people, and has got good blood in his veins."

"I don't see that it would do him much good to have the queen for his aunt, or to go and stay at Windsor Castle, if he had to work hard for his bread all the same," retorted Mrs. Jackson. "What I look to, and what the most of people looks to, is what a man is, not what his relations have been; and if Mr. Barbour be, as I were a-remarking to Mrs. Pratting, nothing-better nor a servant, it seems to me he ought not to put up to gilt ornaments and Geneva velvet chairs, and make a rout about folks, who could buy him and sell him, just looking in at his rooms."

"It is one thing, Mrs. Jackson, to——" began Mrs. Perkins, in defence of her kinsman; but at this moment there appeared a much better advocate, sent by Lawrence, to plead his cause.

"With Mr. Barbour's kindest regards, mum, and to say he hopes you and the child are going on well;" said Mrs. Perkins' maid-of-all-work, entering the room, and presenting to her mistress over the towel-horse a parcel which she held in one corner of her coarse apron, because, as she explained, her hands were black-leady.

"Is he there?　Is he gone?" demanded Mrs. Perkins.

"Yes, ma'am; I asked him if he wouldn't step in, but he said no, that his dinner would be waiting for him;" and Jane, about the tenth servant whose life Mrs. Perkins had made a

weariness since Lawrence first entered Distaff
Yard, lingered in the room, curious to see what
was in the parcel delivered by Mr. Barbour in
person.

"A pair of scissors! oh, dear! Mrs. Nettlefield, have you got a pair of scissors?" exclaimed
Mrs. Perkins, after vainly fighting with the in-
tricacies of a draper's knot. "Run and get a
knife, Jane;" but Jane, whose ingenuity was of
a practical description, had already cut the string
with a pair of snuffers that lay on the mantel-
piece, and four heads were bent inquiringly over
the parcel as Mrs. Perkins unwrapped brown
paper, and blue paper, and white paper, and
finally exposed to view a baby's robe.

"Well I declare!" It was Mrs. Jackson who
broke the silence with this original observation,
and Jane immediately followed suit with, "Oh,
law!" and essayed, having first carefully clothed
her finger and thumb with the skirt of her
dress, to touch the marvellous present.

In a moment Mrs. Perkins' indignation was
excited. "Would she dare to dirty it, to soil the

blessed infant's christening garment?" And thereupon Mrs. Perkins took occasion to rebuke Jane for being an "idle slut," who never got her work done in time; but stood gossiping, and was a disgrace to be seen going to the door in any respectable house.

To which Jane could doubtless have made answer, had she been so disposed, but deeming discretion the better part of valour, and remembering a half-sovereign just presented to her by Mr. Barbour—the much-enduring Ganymede went rather off into ecstasies over the frock, which was—"French, Mrs. Nettlefield—French, every thread of it;" and Mrs. Jackson looked up at the nurse as she said this, as though daring that strong-minded individual to contradict her.

"It would not cost one farthing less than five guineas," went on the soap-boiler's wife, appraising the gift, as such women do,—"not one farthing."

"Did you ever see anything like that, nurse?" asked Mrs. Perkins, exultantly; and the nurse was fain to confess she never had but once, and that was when she was "attending of the lady of Sir 'Umphrey 'All, who was at one time Lord Mayor of London.

"And one of the godmothers, a widow lady as lived at Clapham, and kept a full suite of servants, and drove out regular in her carriage and pair, sent a robe of the same description to the baby, and gave two golden guineas to me," added Mrs. Nettlefield, in slighting reference to Lawrence, who had never thought it needful to present her—no, not with a fourpenny bit.

"Well, I wonder, I do, where that young Barbour gets the money," remarked Mrs. Jackson to her husband, as she bustled about and made tea on her return home.

"What money?" asked Mr. Jackson, from behind his newspaper.

"Why, all he has to spend. I was telling you about his rooms yesterday, though I don't think you heard a word I said, through being fast asleep at the time; but his rooms are splendid— fit for a duke; and to-day, while I was at Mrs. Perkins', there comes a christening-robe as might have done for the Prince of Wales. A fool and his money is soon parted, we know'; but, then, where does he get it? I only hope and trust he is not taking it off poor Mr. Perkins—a sensible, respectable man as you would wish to meet with."

"Mrs. J.," said Mr. Jackson, severely, "do you know what you are talking about?"

"Yes, I do; better than you, at any rate, when you come home from one of your vestry dinners," retorted his better-half.

"Because," calmly went on Mr. Jackson, "it strikes me you don't, when you ask where that young man gets his money, and hopes as he earns it honestly."

"Well, you can't buy furniture that is grand enough for the Pope of Rome, and keep yourself, and pay rent, and washing and mending besides, out of a hundred and fifty pounds a year—and that is every halfpenny, Mrs. Perkins tells me, he earns."

"Well, Mr. Sondes told me, no later than half an hour ago, that there was not a cleverer young

man in London than that same Lawrence Barbour. 'He invented a thing,' he went on, 'which
will save me five hundred a year. I am going to
patent it,' he says, 'and have given him a cheque
for two hundred and fifty pounds——'"

"Lor'-a-mercy! two hundred and fifty pounds
all in a lump!" exclaimed Mrs. Jackson.
"Likely it was out of that he bought the
frock!"

"'And now, I suppose,' says I to Mr. Sondes,"
proceeded Mr. Jackson, taking off his spectacles
and wiping them, and then putting them on
again with sublime deliberation, "'you'll be
taking him into partnership—securing the genius
to the concern.'"

"And I suppose he is," broke in Mrs.
Jackson.

"I think not," answered her husband. "'Mr.
Barbour is a very rising young man,' Mr. Sondes
remarked; 'but there are two sides to every
question, and there are two sides to this;' and if
I'm not greatly mistaken," observed the speaker,
on his own account, "the other side in this case

is the Alwyns. You can just remember what I say, Martha—it is the Alwyns."

"Likely enough; and I would not be one bit surprised if Miss Alwyn chose that frock for him. I don't think it's like a man's buying," in which conjecture Mrs. Jackson chanced, however, to be wrong, for the present was very much like a man's purchase indeed.

"And it is not the first thing Mr. Barbour has invented," went on Mr. Jackson; "nor the first money Mr. Sondes has paid him. So you see there are more ways of getting rich than Mrs. Perkins knows of; and that hundred and fifty pounds may be, after all, but a very small part of the young man's income."

"Well, you do surprise me," said Mrs. Jackson.

"Ay; and I have got something else to tell you that may be a greater surprise," chuckled the soap-boiler. "As I was a-coming down Three-Colt Street to-day, who should I run up against but that young swell we saw the evening we went over to Distaff Yard to inquire about Mr. Barbour after his hurt. I mean a young chap with queer-coloured hair, and quite another cut entirely from Perkins' cousin; you remember him, don't you?"

"Yes; that got a cup of coffee upset over his summer trousers—Ada did it—and who laughed till he was fit to drop when Mrs. Perkins offered to have them sent to the dyers and cleaned for him, and then you told him he ought to send the bill in to Mr. Perkins, and make him pay the damage. 'I don't think my tailor would mind how many cups of coffee were upset, if an arrangement of that kind could be entered into,' I remember he said; 'poor devil! he can scarcely recollect what the colour of my money is like.' A cheery young fellow; what about him, Samuel? what was he doing in Limehouse?"

"I had no notion he would remember me," resumed the soap-boiler; "and, indeed, I could not think for the moment where I had seen him, when he stops me and says—'I am sure you and I have met in some place before, and ought to know each other.' 'Well, I am sure I ought to know you, sir, for your face is familiar; but one sees so many faces in business.' 'Ah ! it wasn't in business you saw mine,' he said. 'Ain't you a friend, or relation, or something of Mr. Perkins in Distaff Yard ? I met you there, and now I have come to live down here beside you.' "

" For any sake, where ? " inquired Mrs. Jackson.

" That is what I was going on to tell you," her husband replied; " you know that ship-building place, with the beautiful house, over the bridge ; well, my gentleman is one of the junior partners in that concern, and is living on the premises. 'I am going to run a race with Barbour,' he says, ' and we are intending to try which of us can die worth half a million.' He is the same as ever. 'Come over and see me,' he remarked, quite friendly. 'Come over and see me promiscuous. Make my respects to your worthy lady ; she is well, I hope ? "

" Quite the gentleman ! " exclaimed Mrs. Jackson, drawing a deep sigh, for she had held her breath during the preceding narrative till she was almost suffocated. "Quite the gentleman !

and I hope, Samuel, you told him we had always a spare knife and fork, and took tea at five, and a bite of supper at nine."

"Yes, I did : and he said he would come over and call upon you, and then, if you gave him permission, he might drop in occasionally. ‘Mrs. Jackson always makes my friends welcome, sir,’ I made free to remark, and at that he laughed, and said, ‘ Of course, all wives do ; but still they like the ceremony of being consulted, nevertheless ; ’ not a bad hit, I thought,—not by no means."

Whatever Mrs. Jackson thought of the hit, it detracted somewhat from her admiration of Mr. Percy Forbes. "Likely as not," she decided, " he is one of them young jackanapeses who think to wind women round their fingers like a skein of silk. He'll not find me one of the soft ones," she mentally affirmed ; but yet, when the young man fulfilled his promise, and called upon her ; when he sat in her best parlour and would not "lay down his hat during the whole visit,—no, not trust it out of his hand, let her say what she liked;" when he discoursed to her about Lime-house and his new home, and criticised the clergyman, and talked about business "as sensible like as her husband," and condoled with her on the loss of her children, and promised to send her round some flowers out of his own conservatory, and asked her to come and see the view of the river from his lawn—Mrs. Jackson was enchanted.

"Now that is the kind of young man for my money," she remarked, in a moment of unguarded confidence to Mr. Sondes. "I was just saying to Samuel, that if I was a young gurl and single, I would give Mr. Forbes no rest till he married me."

"How fortunate it is, then, for Mr. Forbes that you are neither," Mr. Sondes replied, and this reply Mrs. Jackson subsequently repeated to Percy Forbes, who declared his view of the matter to be " widely different."

"God only knows how you can endure those people," observed Lawrence Barbour to him one day.

"My dear fellow, variety is charming," answered Mr. Forbes. "It is well for a man to see a little of all sorts; and as Providence has cast my lot due east, I am determined to make the best of the dispensation."

"If any body had left me eight thousand pounds, I would have seen Limehouse at the devil before coming to live in it," said Lawrence.

"Well, I was going to the devil," retorted Mr. Forbes, "and I thought if ever I meant to turn and go the other road, it was time for me to do so. Had I stayed at the West-end, I should have been in as bad a plight as ever before two years were over; but now, Mr. Barbour, now I am going to try to beat you."

"No great trouble for you to do that, with all the money on your side," was the reply.

"And all the cleverness on yours," returned Percy Forbes; and with that they parted.

END OF VOL. I.

www.ingramcontent.com/pod-product-compliance
Lightning Source LLC
Chambersburg PA
CBHW031138120726
47905CB00006B/1727